THE EMOTIONS

Also by Jean-Philippe Toussaint

Monsieur
Camera
Self-Portrait Abroad
The Truth about Marie
Reticence
Urgency and Patience
Soccer

THE EMOTIONS

JEAN-PHILIPPE TOUSSAINT

Translated from the French by
Mark Polizzotti

OTHER PRESS | NEW YORK

Originally published in French as *Les Émotions* in 2020 by Les Éditions de Minuit, Paris

Title-page illustration by the author.

Production editor: Yvonne E. Cárdenas
Text designer: Patrice Sheridan
This book was set in Janson MT Pro by Alpha Design & Composition of Pittsfield, NH.

10 9 8 7 6 5 4 3 2 1

Printed in the United States of America on acid-free paper. For information write to Other Press LLC, 267 Fifth Avenue, 6th Floor, New York, NY 10016. Or visit our Web site: www.otherpress.com

Library of Congress Cataloging-in-Publication Data
Names: Toussaint, Jean-Philippe, author. | Polizzotti, Mark, translator.
Title: The Emotions / Jean-Philippe Toussaint ; translated from the French by Mark Polizzotti.
Other titles: Émotions. English
Description: New York : Other Press, 2025.
Identifiers: LCCN 2025011640 (print) | LCCN 2025011641 (ebook) | ISBN 9781635422160 (paperback) | ISBN 9781635422177 (ebook)
Subjects: LCGFT: Novels.
Classification: LCC PQ2680.O86 E4613 2025 (print) | LCC PQ2680.O86 (ebook) | DDC 843/.914—dc23/eng/20250314
LC record available at https://lccn.loc.gov/2025011640
LC ebook record available at https://lccn.loc.gov/2025011641

Publisher's Note
This is a work of fiction. Names, characters, places, and incidents either are the product of the author's imagination or are used fictitiously.

I know from where I come,
if not to where I go.

—VICTOR HUGO

I

IT HAD BEEN SWELTERING IN BRUSSELS that day. Diane and I were in the final hours of our life together. We hadn't spoken in weeks. Our marriage, which had lasted ten years, was ending in coldness and resentment. It was June 23, 2016, the day of the Brexit referendum in the UK. That evening, a violent storm broke out over the city, bringing torrential rains. I can still see myself in the living room of the apartment on Rue de Belle-Vue, watching the deluge fall outside the bay windows. The willow branches twisted in the wind. Sometimes a bolt of lightning zigzagged across the sky, and you could hear the rumble of thunder in the distance, past the Ixelles Ponds. Diane was sitting behind me in the darkened living room, leafing silently through a magazine on the sofa. She got up and I heard her move down the hall toward the bedroom. It was our last night together in that apartment—I had already arranged to move into a new place.

I heard the results of the British referendum only the next day, on the radio. I had a meeting at the European Commission first thing in the morning. Afterward, walking out of the Berlaymont, I crossed Rue de la Loi with a few colleagues to go to the Justus Lipsius building across the way. At the time, the Justus Lipsius was the only headquarters of the Council of the European Union; the new Europa building by Philippe Samyn—the famous hollowed-out glass cube that shines at night in the heart of the European Quarter—wouldn't be put into service until early the following year. There was much more animation than usual in the lobby of the Justus Lipsius. We saw TV crews and dozens of reporters hurrying toward the press room. I can still recall the entrance of the European Council president that day. Preceded by a ferment of counselors and security agents, his resolute silhouette marched forward on the red carpet, past the row of European flags. His expression was grim, his demeanor solemn. He climbed onto the stage and began speaking with unusual emotion. I am fully aware of the grave and even tragic magnitude of the moment we're living through, he said. It's a historic moment, but not a time to react hysterically. The last few years have been the most difficult of our history, but I want to reassure everyone that we are prepared to confront this adverse situation, and I'm reminded of what my father used to say: "What doesn't kill you makes you stronger." I watched the European Council president speak from the podium. At the moment he evoked his father, a veil of shyness floated across his eyes, gone in an instant. He gave a brief smile, the smile of an adult man mentioning his father in public, with all it implies of discretion, respect, and filial piety, and I couldn't help thinking about my own father, Jean-Yves Detrez, who had himself been a European commissioner once upon a time. Since I had learned about the "Leave" victory in the

British referendum, I couldn't help thinking how he must feel. His world, the world he had always known, was faltering. Crises were accumulating in Europe, populism was on the rise, everywhere, inexorably. The humanism that my father had always zealously defended seemed in worse shape than ever. Brexit was only the latest manifestation—the most spectacular, the most drastically unexpected—of this poisonous decay.

How deeply can we forget what happens to us? I might never have asked myself that question if, months later, I hadn't found a compromising photo on my phone. I was on a train. I had attended a futurology conference in Paris that morning and was returning to Brussels that same evening, round trip in one day. It had been a long journey and I was tired. I was letting the train rock me to sleep. Nestled in my seat, I was flipping distractedly through the images on my phone when I happened across the photo of a half-naked young woman. The poorly focused image had been taken that summer in a hotel room while I was away at a futurology retreat at Hartwell House, outside of London. I no longer remembered the exact circumstances in which the photo had been taken. I only remembered spending the end of the evening with that woman and taking the majestic staircase of Hartwell House with her very late that night, but I didn't recall what happened next, or rather, after a certain point, my memories dissolved in the haze of an overly boozy evening. Still, no doubt that the photo had been taken in a room at Hartwell House, and clearly by me, since I had just discovered it, to my surprise and embarrassment, on my own phone—which seemed to put the lie to my hazy memory.

For several years, my friend and colleague Peter Atkins had been organizing the Hartwell House Gatherings, futurology retreats at which the participants—political officials, international analysts, experts—met for a week in the sumptuous setting of the Hartwell estate to forecast the future together. For me, who dealt with it on a daily basis as part of my job at the European Commission, the future was a purely abstract notion, which I was able to model and express through figures. But while I had undeniable mastery over the future in my professional life, I realized that, in my private life, it had been some time since I exerted any control whatsoever. My marriage to Diane was crumbling, we were having difficulties that I couldn't see our way out of. For me, the future had become irremediably opaque. I didn't have the tools necessary to imagine what would become of my love story with Diane. It was enough to make you think that futurology is useless in matters of the heart—or that there is no method in love.

When I began to take a professional interest in the future, in the 1990s, I quickly understood that there was an abyss between two notions that might seem related, even identical, but that are in fact quite distinct: *public future* and *private future.* The knowledge or exploration of a public future, which is at the core of my professional activities, is a full-scale discipline, much like statistics or demographics, with specific methodological techniques and tools. When it's practiced according to the rules, futurology allows you to spot the major changes quietly fermenting in a society before they burst out into the open, and thus to anticipate the great evolutions just ahead. Whereas the desire, or the fantasy, of knowing one's private future is more in the realm of spiritualism or clairvoyance—at which point, you might as well consult tarot cards or a crystal ball. Anyway, do we really want to know what the days or weeks ahead have in store for us? Do we want to be told what will become of us in the short or long term, considering that the most momentous things we could learn would be either that we're going to die soon or that we're about to have a new amorous or sexual adventure? Sex and death: nothing matters more to us, when it's about ourselves.

In the summer of 2016, I attended Peter Atkins's futurology retreat at Hartwell House. For those few days, the future was our main preoccupation, and we framed it with expert care. We probed it in small groups, at conference tables draped in green baize. We auscultated it with infinite precaution, to build exploratory scenarios representing possible outcomes. I'd known Peter forever; for almost twenty years, we'd been frequenting the *terra incognita* of strategic forecasting and exploring its last uncharted steppes. In the early 2000s, Peter had joined the staff of the Government Chief Scientific Adviser in London, who advised the prime minister on matters of technology. He had been tasked with creating the first futurology unit within that agency. And so Peter had trained himself, on the job, in the most sophisticated techniques of the discipline and had gotten to know most of the politicians, military officials, and upper functionaries working in the field in England.

After that, experts from other countries, who wanted to create their own futurology groups in their homelands, had come to London to see how it worked, and that was how Peter had become an indispensable personality in the small and very restricted world of strategic forecasting. In 2011, Peter had left his job in the British administration to go out on his own, and had founded the Hartwell House Gatherings Association. The association's flagship event was the summer futurology retreat. Beginning with the very first session, Peter had instituted the radical idea of live challenges. The principle was to have each year a challenge to meet in real time, a general interest topic on which the participants could work over the five days of the retreat. In 2016, the Hartwell House Gathering was held in early July, barely more than a week after the Brexit referendum.

On Monday, July 4, 2016, I boarded the early-morning train in Brussels, bound for London. At the Gare du Midi, I was to meet my friend Viswanathan Ajit Pai, who works with me at the European Commission. Viswanathan was part of the Hartwell House group, and we had decided to travel together. In the Eurostar, we found an empty foursome of seats and settled in, unfolding our newspapers and placing our laptops on the shelves. Viswanathan, comfortably ensconced in his seat, had opened the *Financial Times*, whose salmon-colored pages he turned carefully in a muffled crinkling of newsprint. Shortly after we pulled out, we were served a nice breakfast. Viswanathan was upset, as was I, by the results of the referendum, but he didn't look like he would let himself be defeated by it. On the contrary, enjoying his breakfast, delighting in the pastries and fruit yogurts (his and mine, which I had gladly passed to him), he instead launched into a vibrant retrospective homage to the England he'd known as a student at Cambridge in the early 1990s. You know, back then, it was a really stimulating environment, he said, an atmosphere of free thought and intellectual curiosity. People were talking about the new internationalism. Back then, Great Britain was open to other cultures. That was when you started to be able to eat well in England, with good wines, fine cheeses, excellent olive oil. English society seemed to breathe differently; there was an extraordinary openness to the outside world. According to Viswanathan, things had started to go downhill in the early 2000s, and the financial crisis of 2008 didn't help. Grafted onto those early days of recession were an anti-immigrant rhetoric and the unleashing of populist anti-European journalism. Add to that a fair amount of cynicism and two or three sorcerer's apprentices, Viswanathan concluded, and there was little wonder about the reasons for Brexit (and he finished off my cherry yogurt while glancing pensively through the train window).

Upon our arrival in London, imagine my surprise when Viswanathan Ajit Pai abandoned me without further ado in the arrivals hall of St. Pancras, saying he had a meeting at a lawyer's office in Kensington and would join us at Hartwell House the next day. He vanished into a taxi, and I was left on my own to change stations and board the train for Aylesbury. Once at Hartwell House, I was shown to my room on the third floor, a spacious, elegant accommodation with period furnishings. The drapes and bedspread shimmered in tones of jonquil, narcissus, and pastel green. I washed my hands under the antique copper faucets of the sink and went down to lunch. I walked through the ground floor, admiring as I went the rococo marble mantelpieces and master paintings that decorated the walls of the grand wood-paneled entrance hall. In the dining room, four round tables, each able to accommodate ten or twelve persons, were set with white cloths and silver tableware. The room boasted a very high ceiling and four French doors opening onto a park. Some fifteen people were already present, seated or helping themselves to the buffet. I knew many of them by sight, but didn't see any friends per se among the attendees; Viswanathan had stayed in London and Peter Atkins must have been meeting with his colleagues to prepare for the beginning of the retreat. As often when arriving in an unknown place, I felt self-conscious. I headed for the buffet, took a large plate, and started to serve myself. Not all the attendees had arrived yet, some had already finished lunch and were having coffee, others had barely begun eating. I found a place at a table where seven or eight others were already seated and ate in silence, listening distractedly to the conversations around me. Often, in public—and our futurology conferences were no exception—one person stands out by being more arrogant than the others, some know-it-all who feels no compunctions about contradicting his tablemates. I immediately spotted one such person at our table. Still fairly young, under forty, stocky, with broad shoulders, striped shirt, suspenders, and a voice like a megaphone. No matter where you were, inescapably, his voice boomed from afar and assaulted your ears. Moreover, his voice was not only loud, but distinctly grating. The guy apparently had an irrepressible need to affirm his superiority over everyone else, though it was hard to tell on what that superiority might rest. He wasn't talking to his neighbors so much as lecturing them. He had cut short any attempt to start other conversations, monopolizing the entire table and reserving his most penetrating gazes for the young woman who had sat next to me, not to seek her approval but to favor her with a discreet flirtatious tribute. I didn't know the woman's name (it was written on her badge, but I wasn't about to lean over her chest to read it), nor did I know what exactly she did, only that she was Finnish, and that I had already seen her at a futurology colloquium in the United States. The man across the table kept on with his perorations. I later learned that his name was Scott Adams. He had a certain presence, but there was something unpleasant about him, even vaguely obscene, such as his way of mashing bread dough between his fingers and gluttonously lifting food to his mouth. He also had the tic of punctuating a sentence or underscoring his dicta by touching the people around him, gripping with a vicelike hand the arm of the woman next to him, all the while continuing to stare (for he had several irons in the fire) at the Finnish woman sitting next to me. He was the complete opposite of the neighbor on my right, a Japanese man as reserved as I was, who, after having discreetly slipped into his seat, said not a word and kept his eyes lowered, endeavoring to take up as little space as possible. The only time he spoke to me, in an almost inaudible voice, was to ask me to pass the bread, practically apologizing for the brazenness of his request.

On the topic of Brexit, which was on everyone's mind, Scott Adams, who claimed to have the ears of the bigwigs and must have had his entrees with the upper crust, began telling us the story of the Pizza Summit. I had already heard rumors about this pseudo-meeting in an airport, but nothing truly verified. The story went that the decision to hold a referendum on whether Britain should remain in the European Union was made in a pizzeria in Chicago's O'Hare Airport as the British delegation was returning from a NATO summit. The main actors in the scene Scott Adams described to us were the British prime minister and his secretary of foreign affairs, whom, with exasperating familiarity, he called by their first names (Dave and William), as if these were close friends of his who had simply goofed, albeit goofed badly, and he was relating an amusing anecdote. Telling us the story, which he surely didn't know firsthand and whose authenticity was dubious, he delivered every detail of the scene as if he'd been present, adding the purely rhetorical warning that we not repeat it to anyone. It had to remain *off the record*, as he put it. And, lowering his voice while motioning conspiratorially for us to draw closer, he apprised us that the only way Dave had found that evening to preserve the unity of the Conservative Party during the election campaign of 2015 was to promise a referendum on the European Union. It's unbelievable! he said. Can you imagine, that disastrous referendum, which has entailed the collapse of the pound sterling and will no doubt lead Great Britain into an unprecedented crisis, was decided by three or four politicians sitting idly around a pizza in Terminal 3 at O'Hare. *Capriccio* pizza, no doubt! he chortled, and he snatched up his neighbor's napkin to smugly wipe his lips (I caught the neighbor's horrified glance, who didn't know whether she should point out that it was *her* napkin he'd grabbed). Whether or not the anecdote of the Pizza Summit is apocryphal, what made his story so repugnant was not so much the tone of inner-circle snobbery with which he'd told it as the casual familiarity with which he'd mentioned the protagonists (even if, of course, the British political leaders implicated in Brexit were far from blameless).

Scott Adams kept speechifying about the state of the world. It was as if he needed to systematically defend a position that was the opposite of commonly held opinions. It was an approach that could, intellectually, have a certain legitimacy when it came to playing devil's advocate in order to study a question from every angle, but which often led him into deliberately inflammatory oratorical contortions. Most historians date the beginning of the twentieth century to 1914, don't you know, he explained to us, sipping his coffee while holding the saucer. Well, for historians of the future, it should have been much simpler, at least in theory, since everyone agrees that the twenty-first century started in 2001, with 9/11. But, he went on, setting his cup down on the table, it might well be that another date might compete with 2001, and this date—he paused a moment to build suspense—is 2016! Yes, this very year! You see, 2016 is a pivotal year, one world ending and a new era beginning. With Brexit, a page is being turned. But 2016 isn't only about Brexit, he added. This will also be the year when Trump is elected president! For it will indeed be Trump who wins in November! There were a few snickers around the table, some shrugs, a murmur of dissent. I'm serious, he said. As unlikely as that victory might seem today, it is not impossible. And this is not fortune-telling, but the result of well-documented analysis (the filmmaker Michael Moore, by the way, reached the same conclusions as me, he told us, snatching up a petit four from the dessert tray). I watched Scott Adams from across the table and was irritated by the sensationalizing prediction he'd just made, which bore no relation to futurology, was even its opposite. This Scott Adams had clearly understood nothing about futurology; it was high time he attended a retreat such as this, to learn about our discipline's ethics and goals. The irony of the whole thing (but I hadn't known this at the time) was that *he* was the expert invited to teach us the method to be used at Hartwell House; he was the famous Scott Adams whom Peter had recruited that year to handle the methodological portion of our retreat. Meanwhile, not yet aware of who he was, I kept listening to him pontificate. With great self-assurance, all the while plucking petit fours from the tray, he listed the various objective parameters that would, he said, explain Trump's victory in November. With the same rhetoric, and the same reservations ("I'm not saying this is necessarily what will happen, merely that we should not consider the hypothesis impossible"), he announced, for the following year, the triumph of the populists in the Netherlands and the victory of the far-right candidate in the French presidential elections, before ending, with a theatrical flourish, on a quote that he attributed to Kurt Vonnegut (and woe betide you if you didn't know who Kurt Vonnegut was): "History is merely a list of surprises. It can only prepare us to be surprised yet again." It was a bit much for me, so I got up from the table without having coffee and went back to my room—besides, the petit fours were all gone.

It was very dark in my room, and I could hear the rain beating against the windows. I tried to turn on the bedside lamp, but it had a complicated mechanism: I spent a long time searching for the switch, which ended up being not on the cord but under the light bulb, and which you didn't raise or lower but rotated to the right (those English, I swear). I took a short nap, then went back downstairs a little before three o'clock. I spotted Peter Atkins scurrying around, papers in hand, welcoming the new arrivals while encouraging the attendees to head toward the annex for the inaugural session. We left the hotel and walked up the path in small clusters under a threatening sky. The rain had ceased for the moment, and the wet branches dripped in the humidity. There was an attentive effervescence around Scott Adams; several people were following him, surrounding him, crowding into his wake. I had stayed behind, silent, in my corner. It was then that I noticed the presence of a young woman walking on her own, holding a satchel, whom I hadn't yet spotted among the participants. She was wearing a raw silk blouse and a mohair vest, a string of pearls around her neck. She radiated a discreet elegance, a charm, a reserve that immediately held my attention. I'm not sure what attraction is based on, but while most of the men present seemed drawn to the Finnish woman, whose appearance, it's true, stood out in our austere assembly, with her long legs and fuchsia spike-heel pumps, personally I was more attracted to that self-effacing young woman. I didn't dare engage her in conversation, and contented myself with following her at a distance, not letting her out of my sight. I walked behind her into the James Gibbs Room, where the opening session would be held. Each place at the large U-shaped table had been provided with a notepad, pencil, and the program for the retreat. Several people were already seated; others chatted informally while waiting for the session to begin. I hedged for a moment, standing near the woman with the mohair vest, hesitating, distractedly leafing through a program that I had picked up from the table, before taking a seat next to her.

For the inaugural session, Peter Atkins had gone to an outside facilitator, a psychologist who had developed some innovative approaches to group communication. Rather than letting the participants introduce themselves one by one in classic fashion, "My name is So-and-so, I work for the Such-and-such organization" (all that information, she told us, was in the pamphlet each of us had received), she suggested that as a way of getting to know one another, we proceed immediately to a first exercise, called Tell the Story of Your Name. It was an exercise she had borrowed from the work of Puanani Burgess, a consultant and trainer from Hawaii. These days, she explained, we typically introduce ourselves only with our first and last names, without realizing what invisible riches they contain. What this exercise proposed was to tell the history of our name, relate its origins. In fact, when we tell the story of our names, it brings to light a large part of our personal history. She invited us to do the exercise in pairs, for ten minutes, after which we'd each relate our findings about our partner to the group at large. Understood? There was a brief flurry in the room, we turned toward our neighbors to find out who our teammate would be. As luck would have it, after gauging the distribution of seats around the table, I realized that I'd be paired with the woman in the mohair vest. She must have seen it too, as we smiled at each other, a bit shyly. Around us, a number of teams had already gotten to work, we could hear whispering in the room, some were already jotting down notes on their pads. My neighbor picked up her pencil and invited me to go first (I couldn't believe it, not only was this seductive young woman asking me about myself, but was preparing to take notes—notes!—on what I would say). I introduced myself: My name is Jean Detrez, I work for the European Commission. I explained that my family was Belgian, but my name came from the north of France. I watched her writing it down on her pad. My father's paternal grandfather was French, and he was notable for having disappeared during the First World War. No one knows what became of him, only that he went off to war in August 1914 and never returned. Was he killed in combat? Did he desert? Did he take the opportunity to start a new life with another woman? We had no clue about his fate, but family legend had it that *he* was the Unknown Soldier buried under the Arc de Triomphe. She looked at me quizzically, as if wondering whether I had made that up (but who could make up such a story?). Then it was her turn to take the plunge. My name is Enid Eelmäe, she told me, and I'm Estonian. I raised my eyes toward her. I asked her to repeat her name so that I could write it down, and it gave me infinite pleasure to hear her pronounce her name again, Enid Eelmäe, in her melodious voice. I was under her spell. She didn't know why her parents had named her Enid, which was hardly a typical forename in Estonia. The only Enid she knew of was the English writer Enid Blyton, author of *The Famous Five* and *The Secret Seven.* When I heard her pronounce those titles, which I immediately placed in my memory by translating them into French (*Le Club des cinq*! *Le Clan des sept*!), it was as if my entire childhood suddenly made an improbable, brilliant irruption in the James Gibbs Room. And even though I had forgotten nearly everything about the plots of those books, the places where I'd read them remained indelibly fixed in my memory. Enid Eelmäe continued her story. Her family name, Eelmäe, meant "first mountain" or "fore-hill" in Estonian. The name had a long history, she explained. First, you had to know that, before 1819, there were very few peasants in Estonia who had a name, so much so that "Estonian" and "peasant" were practically synonymous. It was only with the abolition of serfdom that the educated classes, the pastors, the Baltic barons, had started giving the peasants names. Sometimes the nobles issued them strange ones (strange, even in Estonian, she said with a smile), or else the pastor, who didn't understand Estonian very well, used a mangled spelling. It was only at the time of the first Republic of Estonia, between the two world wars, that things had begun to standardize. There was a great campaign of *Estonianization* in the 1930s, and it was only then that her family name became Eelmäe. Before it was Estonianized, do you know what our name was? she asked. I looked at her and shook my head, with a gentle smile: How could I have known? You'd hardly believe it, she said. And do you know how I found out? I again shook my head, curious to know the rest. It was through August Eelmäe, a famous actor in Estonia. I realized, when looking into the family name, that *his* name, before being Eelmäe, had been Eiffel! Like Gustave. Gustave? I said. Yes, Gustave Eiffel, as in the Eiffel Tower! It was only in 1936 that the actor's parents decided to change Eiffel into Eelmäe. And it's probably the same thing that happened with my name, I became Eelmäe, when originally I was an Eiffel. You thus see before you a putative descendant of the builder of the Eiffel Tower! she said with a laugh. I smiled back. The exercise was coming to an end, and the psychologist, who had stood back up, came through the room to ask for a first duo to report its results. I was still writing down my notes, but it would soon be our turn (I wasn't worried, though: we had both the Arc de Triomphe and the Eiffel Tower on our side).

After a break, Peter Atkins took over to lead the second session of the afternoon. Wearing a gray suit and dark tie, he stood quietly beneath a projection screen and waited for the last participants, making their way along the table, to take their seats. I knew certain deadpan aspects of Peter's personality, his nonchalance, his phlegmatic eccentricity, his taste for wry jokes, which he used to make while exhaling the smoke from his cigarillo with placid mischief, stocking feet on the coffee table, back when we would share a thirty-year-old Scotch in the library of his place in Camden Town ("Never put ice in whiskey, you lout!"). But for today, Peter had smoothed all the rough edges from his behavior. Had I not known him personally, I could easily have been mistaken about his character. I also noted that he was a very self-assured public speaker, almost authoritarian.

Since the end of the Second World War, he told us, Europe has known two great cycles: a cycle that we might call *progressive*, as regards values and human rights, until the end of the 1970s; and a *liberal* cycle, which lasted more or less until the financial crisis of 2008. With Brexit, we appear to have entered a third cycle, a *populist* one, expressed as a new mistrust of elites and of representative democracy. Added to this is the fact that, over the past several years, numerous crisis spots and unstable regions have sprung up on Europe's borders—Ukraine, Crimea, Turkey, Libya—such that our increasingly fragile continent might seem encircled by a ring of fire. You all know the Johnny Cash song (to everyone's surprise, he began singing the chorus into the mic, slightly bending his knees and swaying in time with the cord: *And it burns, burns, burns! The ring of fire, the ring of fire!*). Then, imperturbably, resuming his explanations as if nothing had happened, he announced that this year's live challenge would be about the European Union's foreign policy. What he proposed was for us to reevaluate and reimagine together the international strategy of the EU, taking into account new regional instabilities in the time of Brexit. As you are all aware, he said, we always try, here at Hartwell House, to broach topics that are not yet resolved, still in flux. I am therefore submitting an open question for your insights. To help you arrive at answers, I've put together a program of lectures and conferences with speakers who will debate the topics related to our live challenge. As for the methodology, I am especially proud to announce that the expert who will be working with us at this year's retreat is Scott Adams. And it was only at that moment, as the expert in question rose from his seat and bowed his head at the applause, that I realized that the guy in the striped shirt and suspenders who had exasperated me since my arrival at Hartwell House was the same Scott Adams, the famous, provocative Scott Adams, the rising star of futurology, whom until now I'd known only by reputation. Here I was, applauding Scott Adams (though only with my fingertips, the way you applaud half-heartedly, trying to make as little sound as possible and to leave off as soon as you can).

After Peter's introductory remarks, we immediately got down to brass tacks. Collectively, we drew up an initial list of the major variables that could affect the EU's foreign policy over the coming years, our goal being to envision the situation around 2030. Each time someone in the room made a suggestion, it was discussed by the rest of the assembly and, if it was retained, Peter wrote it down in blue marker on a pad on the easel, gradually filling the sheet. After about an hour, we had identified no fewer than twenty-five variables. At the end of the session, based on these variables, we had managed to define two main throughlines that could have an impact on the future of the EU's policy. The first was "the status of resources," which could evolve toward abundance (the plus side) or depletion (the minus side). The second was "the status of values," which, in the next fifteen years, could go in one of two opposite directions: a rise in societal values that were generous and progressive (the plus side), or a hardening of conservative, inward-looking trends, which were already evident in many countries (the minus side). At that point came the first confrontation, though still with kid gloves on, between Scott Adams and Peter, which prefigured the toxic relations they'd maintain for most of the retreat. Scott Adams interrupted Peter, asking by what criteria he took the liberty of assigning a "plus" to progressive values and a "minus" to conservative ones. It was perhaps a reasonable question, but it was also indelicate, and certainly not very diplomatic, to nitpick with Peter as of the very first session, especially on a point of methodology. In a glacial tone, Peter answered that it was not his intention to do that. But it's what you did do, said Scott Adams. Visibly annoyed, and to put an end to the internal debate, Peter added curtly that it was a simple convention (and in no way a value judgment, everyone being free to assign positive or negative status to whatever values they chose, according to their personal convictions), but that in order to move forward, he had adopted what seemed to him the most intuitive option, so that we might establish four possible scenarios, assembling two by two the different poles in every possible combination.

The implicit understanding I had begun sharing with Enid Eelmäe that afternoon in the inaugural session continued the rest of the day. At dinner, walking into the dining room, we naturally sat together, and over dinner I told her that I had worked at the European Commission with an Estonian colleague, Siim Kallas (at the time, I was in charge of interinstitutional relations at the Directorate General for Mobility and Transport, or DG MOVE). Eating elegantly under the sparkling chandeliers of the Hartwell House dining room, Enid answered that Siim Kallas was a major figure in Estonia, a prominent personality in public life. After taking a sip of white wine, she added that he would no doubt represent his party, the Reform Party, in the next presidential elections (and it occurred to me to ask Scott Adams—whose bombastic voice had been hovering over us from the next table since the start of dinner—which candidate would win the Estonian elections, since he surely had an opinion on the matter). After dinner, as the various members spread into parlors or went up to their rooms, Enid and I went out to the terrace to get some air. It had stopped raining, and I proposed a walk in the park.

We headed off together over the lawn. The air was cool, and the smell of damp grass rose in the darkness. We crossed a bridge straddling a still pond, then continued our route along a path that curved between hundred-year-old trees. After barely five minutes, we could already no longer see the hotel lights, nor any light at all, only the vast, starry sky stretching above us beyond the treetops. We walked side by side in silence in the dark. We could feel above us the presence of the universe, its light weight, infinite and immaterial. Enid took her phone from her pocket. She stopped in the path and framed the sky, arms raised above her head. When she took the photo, the flash went off, and a streak of white ripped through the darkness, bathing her face and shoulders in light, momentarily freezing her silhouette in its mohair vest among the trees. Then darkness closed in on us again, darker still in that it had just been shot through by the bright flash. I made out Enid next to me, bending over her phone to see what she'd gotten. She moved close to my shoulder to show me the photo with a laugh: there was nothing but a rectangle of yellowish haze. I told her it was next to impossible to photograph the night sky. Even if she had disabled the flash, it was too dark for the sensors to catch anything. I added, resuming our walk, face to the stars, that it was ultimately a privilege reserved for our eyes alone to be able to grasp the splendor of the night sky. She came up to me and we exchanged a look in the darkness, a look that felt full of unspoken promise, a look that lasted a bit longer than it should have, but nothing more, and we walked on. As we headed back, we could see in the distance the lit façade of Hartwell House. The terrace doors had remained open, and there were yellow lights in some of the upstairs windows, suggesting invisible activity in the rooms. Enid walked beside me, eyes lowered. I couldn't deny that, during our walk, when we had been alone in the dark, it had crossed my mind to take her hand, but it had never gone further than that fleeting notion; I had never imagined taking that step other than in my thoughts. We were about to reach the hotel. Enid had gone four or five yards ahead of me and was about to step onto the terrace, and it was then that, on a sudden impulse, I discreetly pulled out my phone and, without even bringing it up to my eyes, keeping it by my hip and framing by instinct in the dark, I took a picture of her, secretly, with pounding heart, like a stolen kiss. When she turned around to wait for me and accompany me into the hotel, all trace of my transgression had vanished; my phone was already back in my pocket. I trembled at the thought of her discovering my subterfuge, but apparently she hadn't noticed a thing. We continued on into the hotel, crossed through a parlor in which several of the retreat attendees were still chatting, and headed up the stairs, where we parted to go to our separate rooms. That night, in bed before going to sleep, I studied the photo I'd taken of Enid. The picture was hazy, grainy, full of static; all you could see was an indistinct, shadowy expanse from which emerged Enid's profile in motion against the hotel terrace. I enlarged her face with my fingers, the better to make out her features. She was unrecognizable in the photo. Only a tiny fragment of her cheek appeared in the shadows, her nose, the arched line of her eyebrow, a small, unruly lock of hair forming a rogue curl on her forehead.

◆

The next day, when we resumed our work in the James Gibbs Room, the configuration had changed. The large U-shaped table had been replaced by four round tables covered in green baize. The seats were unassigned, and I went to sit next to Enid Eelmäe. The morning began with a panel discussion on "means of thinking about the future." After some brief introductory remarks by the panelists, the general discussion started up, which Peter led with his usual aplomb, picking up on the panelists' points and inviting the room to join in. The air conditioning from the ceiling was frigid, and those who had removed their jackets soon put them back on; several women covered their shoulders with shawls. One of Peter's assistants discreetly left the room to go turn off the AC. He came back in, silently closing the door behind him, while the debate continued onstage. Apparently he hadn't succeeded, as everyone in the room was still shivering and looking for extra coverings. Then, at the end of the debate, Peter introduced the morning's two speakers. The first, an English academic of Indian origin, gave a brilliant, concise, well-informed presentation. He spoke of the conceptual differences in futurology between France and the United States. I was on familiar ground. He cited names often ignored by Anglo-American futurology. He spoke briefly and without notes. I myself took some notes while listening to him, something I rarely do, bearing in mind the unwritten rule that one is more liable to take notes when the speaker speaks without any than when he reads his speech. Sadly, this was not the case with the second speaker. I didn't know who he was (his name meant nothing to me), and I'd be unable to say what he was talking about. He looked like a monk, Trappist or Cistercian, with greasy hair in a bowl cut with bangs and a thick nose (you could easily imagine him making his own cheeses). Standing beside the screen, he read his talk in a monotone, juggling awkwardly between his pages and the clicker that controlled his slides. His PowerPoint redundantly echoed his oral presentation, with graphics that were dishearteningly lame, accompanied by dubiously "humorous" captions. Now take Karl Marx, he said, and brought up onscreen an image of a "cool" Karl Marx, fingers in a V-sign like a Japanese tween on social media. The photo had a caption in bright, puffy orange type that blared some hoary cliché of strategic forecasting about desirable futures and hopeful prospects. I exchanged sympathetic glances with Enid, who smiled and rolled her eyes. The talk, as could be expected, was endless (another often observed unwritten rule: the less the speaker has to say, the longer he goes on), but by this time, no one in the room was listening to the Cistercian. We gazed at the walls with their portraits of Buckinghamshire nobles, distractedly consulted our phones on our knees. At the next table, I noticed that the Finnish woman had taken off one of her pumps and was slowly rubbing the side of her foot on the carpet. I looked at her bare foot under the table, nails varnished royal purple, which radiated something troubling and erotic. I picked up the brochure containing the pictures and resumes of the attendees and, reading her bio, I saw that she worked for the Finnish Ministry of Defense, Information Section, which, given the contrast between her appearance and her professional activity, made her painted toes seem even more wanton. A little later—our Trappist, at his screen, still hadn't finished—I happened to notice that one of the participants, at the next table, had gone online and was googling the Finnish woman, looking at photos of her on his laptop (his Mac was on his knees, but I'd caught a glimpse of the screen over his shoulder). As the speaker had already overrun his allotted time by at least five minutes, I saw Peter start to fidget in his chair. He jotted down something on a sheet of paper, stood up, and slid along the walls to place himself in the presenter's line of sight. Peter raised his arms and held the sheet out toward him. The speaker fell silent. He couldn't read the sign, gave Peter a quizzical look. Two minutes, Peter called out, which pulled the attendees from their torpor and generated a few laughs. The presenter, with an innocent grin, thinking he was being laughed *with* rather than *at*, quickly brought his talk to an end with a final joke. What's the difference between diplomats and camels? Camels can drink very little and work for months at a time, while diplomats are able to drink and drink and drink, and never work. Very funny, Peter said icily, and he began to applaud to prevent the speaker from continuing his talk. I added a few lukewarm claps (jokes bore me).

After a twenty-minute break, during which coffee and tea were served in an adjacent salon, the James Gibbs Room hosted Scott Adams's inaugural lecture ("Thinking the Future," the program announced). Peter, in his introduction, said that Scott Adams was no doubt the most promising futurologist of his generation. Scott Adams, remarkably sober, listened with an ambiguous smile. There was something impertinent in his gaze, something malevolent, or at least discourteous. Standing immobile next to Peter, he seemed to be spoiling for a fight or awaiting his moment (as if thinking, "Just you wait"). The minute Peter left him the floor, he took over the space. Striding around the room, mic in hand, he prowled among the tables like a wild beast. He was in his element now. He was doing his show, and you had to admit that he had charisma. But I also soon noticed that things were not going as planned. I learned afterward, in confidence from Peter, that Scott Adams felt the method that had always been taught at Hartwell House was "old school," not to say outdated. But Peter hadn't given in; he wasn't about to change his method on every guest speaker's say-so. He told me that during their preparatory conversations, he'd had to insist vehemently before Scott Adams agreed to teach the Hartwell House method, and only grudgingly at that. Apart from this, Peter had given the man carte blanche to present his experimental new approaches to assessing the future. But once he got started, Scott Adams, perversely, hadn't been able to resist airing his disagreements with Peter and letting the audience know that he utterly disagreed with the method he was being forced to teach. It was thus with acrid sarcasm that he named the four stages of the Hartwell House method—*scoping, ordering, implications, integrating futures*—as if they were four broken-down tractors, and good luck to us all if we tried to use them to explore the fertile fields of strategic forecasting, as he conceived of it. Before getting into the details of each phase, and destroying any illusions we might still harbor about the fruitfulness of any one of them, he took the opportunity to throw a final barb at scenario modeling, even though he knew full well that it was the method Peter was using for the live challenge. Oh, right, scenario modeling? he said with a mocking smile. It's very nice, really—very scholarly, very didactic, with its two main tendencies and its pluses and minuses. All that comes from Shell, as you know, and none of it is very recent. I—and, I don't know, maybe you? he said insolently—I wasn't born at the time, and he began to snicker. He didn't laugh, he didn't smile, he snickered. Life made the man snicker. The Hartwell House method made him snicker. The future made him snicker. And we, of course, sitting there silently, attentive, listening to him religiously, made him snicker, often benevolently, at our pathetic ignorance (toward which he was willing to be indulgent), but sometimes fiercely if anyone asked a question in which he perceived a hint of challenge or criticism. I looked over at Peter wedged into his chair, glowering, unable to react (I could tell he was fuming, on the verge of leaping up to yank the mic from the other man's hand and make a formal rebuttal). The tension in the room was palpable, the atmosphere toxic, and this was only the first lecture. Nor did things get better afterward, far from it. I learned from Peter that the emergency meeting that took place after lunch behind the library's closed doors was especially stormy. Scott Adams looked dumbfounded, couldn't see what he'd done that was so awful. But Peter and his assistants had gotten fed up after some new condescending jibes about them (the more wrongheaded he is, the more arrogant he gets, Peter said), and the falling-out was complete. Peter tried to get rid of him, but couldn't because of his contract, so he and Scott Adams stopped speaking altogether. From then to the end of the retreat, we barely saw Scott Adams on the pathways of Hartwell House. He only showed up for his lectures in the James Gibbs Room (which he'd renamed the Scott Adams Room), arriving late, eccentric and temperamental, to deliver talks that were lackadaisical, brilliant, and out of the ordinary. He spent the rest of his time on the phone. Or we saw him reading Shakespeare, barefoot in a lounge chair on the terrace, or walking in the park surrounded by the dwindling court of his remaining acolytes.

The afternoon was devoted to the live challenge. When, at the beginning of the session, Peter announced the distribution of work groups in the James Gibbs Room—with the notable absence of Scott Adams, who stayed cloistered in his room all afternoon—I realized that it was all the same to me which scenario I was assigned to work on; the only thing I cared about, vain as it might seem, was to be in the same group as Enid Eelmäe. My wish did not come true: Enid was put in the group devoted to the darkest option (conservative values and depleted resources), and I in the rosiest, which was small consolation. The four groups couldn't all work in the James Gibbs Room, as the sound of voices and echoes of conversation would have been too distracting. Only two groups stayed in the room, a third went to the salon where we took tea, and the last, Enid Eelmäe's, was asked to use the benches and coffee tables in the reception hall of the annex, which also housed the entrance to the swimming pool (as such, it wasn't uncommon, Enid told me, that while they were working they would suddenly see a spa guest in a bathrobe and pool shoes squeaking by them on his way to hydrotherapy). As soon as the members were announced for each group, in a cacophony of scraping seats and shuffled papers, our studious assembly undertook its great hubbub of musical chairs. Everyone packed up and headed to his or her assigned place. For me, the migration wasn't very far, only across the room.

My group included a Mexican woman, managing director of the Plan; an American who worked at the Pentagon; an Australian academic; a former Nigerian minister; and a researcher from Brunei. In this sort of grouping, there are always some who are reserved and others who are more talkative and take charge of the conversation: perhaps because they're more used to leading teams, they quickly assert their dominance. In our group, this was the case with Carmen Zúñiga, the Mexican, big dark hair, gold jewelry, flecked linen suit. From the start, since we were supposed to envision a scenario for the year 2030, she asked what subjective perception we might have of 2030. While at first glance it might seem rather distant from 2016, she said, in reality, if we wanted to get an idea of the time distance between now and 2030, we needed only look backward to realize that it was the same distance separating us from 2001. Does 2001 seem that far in the past to you? There was agreement around the table that 2030, despite appearances, was much sooner than it seemed and that it was in no way a phantom or utopian future over which we could have no influence. On the contrary, the seeds of this future were already in our present. Pushing the question further, Carmen Zúñiga suggested that for 2030, Europe could aim to create, in opposition to the "ring of fire" Peter Atkins had mentioned, a "ring of prosperity" that could be realized through policies of targeted aid. Linda Smith, the American, short hair, flowered dress, and glasses, nodded vigorously and rapidly took notes on her pad. She raised her eyes and added that these policies could take inspiration from what the Marshall Plan had been in its day. The Australian academic, sitting next to her, silent and with folded arms, maintained throughout an attitude of skeptical mistrust and seemed to be systematically opposed to everything said at the table. Unlike people who constantly nod to agree with the speaker, he could not help shaking his head imperceptibly. Paying him no heed, Carmen Zúñiga then launched into the main theoretical developments. My thoughts began to drift, and I started looking around the room. My mind wandered at random, and I was only half listening to the statements being made around me. I could have stayed that way for a long time, lost in my reverie, if I hadn't been yanked from my torpor by the sudden arrival of Viswanathan Ajit Pai.

Viswanathan Ajit Pai hadn't even taken the time to check in or drop his bags in his room. He still had his rolling suitcase with him and his backpack on his shoulder and was exactly as I had left him the day before at St. Pancras. He was with Peter Atkins, who entered the room ahead of him. I saw them creeping stealthily toward me, taking care to make no noise so as not to disturb the proceedings. The conversation at our table didn't stop, merely paused for a second, and a slightly flustered Carmen Zúñiga kept speaking while casting furtive glances at the new arrival. Peter leaned down to my ear and explained that Viswanathan would be joining our group. He asked me to bring him up to speed on our work so far. He went off to find him a chair, and Viswanathan took his place at our table, not the least embarrassed, with the ease of a cabinet minister walking into a meeting straight from the airport. He nodded in silent greeting to everyone without interrupting the discussion, and I barely had time to lean over to him to whisper a recap of where we were (despite having no idea myself) than he not only joined in the conversation but took the lead. With his hawklike eyes, quick mind, and the eel-like suppleness he deployed in public, he had grasped straightaway the substance of our debate and become its new foreperson, while not entering into rivalry with Carmen Zúñiga. On the contrary, their talents were complementary, they seemed to have a mutual appreciation, and it was now a two-headed leader who piloted our work. Viswanathan had immediately removed his jacket, which he draped over the chair behind him by feel; practically vibrating with enthusiasm, he predicted that, in the optimistic perspective we were envisioning, with the expected progress in artificial intelligence, deep learning, and neural networks, by 2030 Europe would become a mythical and fully automated society, in which a number of policy decisions could be handled by algorithms.

And so we met every afternoon to continue our work. I don't know if it was related to Scott Adams's fall from grace, but it felt as if our quest was lacking in direction, that we were developing our scenario without methodological guidance. Ultimately, the exercise was more like a general discussion about what society might look like in 2030, in which a few dominant themes emerged under the joint leadership of Carmen Zúñiga and Viswanathan Ajit Pai. Linda Smith also contributed to our septet, and I occasionally emitted some informed comments of my own (on the blockchain of the quantum computer, for instance), to let my voice be heard. The other participants only listened in silence to the musical themes we produced, the arabesques we deployed, the complex, refined intellectual volutes we elaborated (in this regard, Viswanathan Ajit Pai's virtuosity was unparalleled). The Australian academic, arms still folded, continued to display his attitude of reserved disapproval, while the researcher from Brunei, behind her veil, said not a word.

On the second day, a disagreement broke out at our table. We were convinced that by 2030, Europe would become a global reference in matters of green economy. A circular economy would attain the utopian goal of zero emissions through widespread recycling, and we were reviewing the various domains that might be affected, contemplating even the most outlandish proposals, when the Australian academic, who had been listening to our speculations without unfolding his arms, finally unclenched his teeth to say, "And what else besides? Why not recycle the dead, while we're at it!" His remark had been like a wet blanket. There was a moment of silence, soon broken by Viswanathan Ajit Pai. Right! Right! he cried out, bouncing up and down in his chair. Why not? And he put the hypothesis on the table, suggesting we take the idea of recycling the dead literally. Whenever someone died, there could in fact be a selective triage to harvest the internal organs most in demand, such as kidneys, corneas, pancreases. Carmen Zúñiga said the proposal was audacious, but it was in the spirit of what they were after when developing such scenarios. We shouldn't hesitate to exaggerate, push the envelope. After thinking about it, and with all due seriousness, she said she was in favor of including the proposal in our scenario. I agreed with her, as did Linda Smith. In a shy but firm voice, the researcher from Brunei said she considered the proposition "unseemly." There were two opposing camps at our table. We then turned to Onyekwere Chikwere, the Nigerian ex-minister, who, shrewdly, with eyes asquint, was awaiting his turn. Since the start of our discussions, he had remained aloof and detached, even somewhat haughty, a man of few words, who only spoke to give the final say, as if all decisions were his to make. He took his time to reflect, sitting immobile, hands crossed under his chin—everyone turned to him in anticipation—and ended up agreeing with us. Thank you, Mister Minister, Viswanathan said, and he quickly approved the proposal's inclusion in our report, jotting it on his notepad. (I don't know whether he intended any sarcasm in his "Thank you, Mister Minister," but it struck me as both formally irreproachable and slyly impertinent.)

Leaving the James Gibbs Room that afternoon, Viswanathan took me aside in the pathway as we headed back to the hotel and confessed that, whenever he took part in this kind of group workshop, he always felt as if he were in a role-playing exercise. You know the English expression *suspension of disbelief*? he said. It's something well known in theater studies, a moment when you let go your critical spirit and completely enter into the storyline. Well, that's exactly how it is with futurology. Sometimes, I feel like if someone were looking in from the outside and heard some of our hypotheses, they'd really wonder what we were smoking. A classic example, he added as we walked into the hotel, is the scene from *Richard III*, you know, when Richard, having just killed his brother, turns to Lady Anne, his brother's wife, to confess his love for her. He stopped in the lobby to act out the scene for me (he took on the role of Richard and addressed me as if I were Lady Anne). He admits he killed his brother, then practically in the same breath says he wants to marry her! he cried. We were standing facing one another in the hotel lobby. Obviously it's not at all believable, and yet the audience buys it, the scene has enough dramatic force for the spectator to suspend his critical judgment about the implausibility of the situation. Let's go get a beer, he said, adding, as he dragged me toward the bar, that suspension of disbelief was a central notion in forecasting. When you formulate scenarios, you necessarily have to set aside a lot of disbelief, otherwise there's no point. He ordered two beers at the bar and explained that this voluntary suspension of incredulity was basically an experiment in cognitive simulation, which consisted in agreeing to explore every facet of a fiction that might at first seem unbelievable, in the knowledge that the discoveries we come up with might ultimately have practical application in real life, once we've regained our critical spirit. In the final account, he said, but then stopped. He raised his glass, stared at it for a moment while pursuing his thoughts, and let the matter drop. He took a sip of beer and set his glass back on the bar with a sigh of satisfaction. A fine mustache of foam was sketched across his lip. I told him that I, too, these last two days, had pushed my critical sense to the back burner.

On the afternoon of the last day, the participants gathered once more in the James Gibbs Room to present our findings from the live challenge. Entering the room, I went to join the members of my group. All the tables were filled, and there was a din of conversations as we waited for the session to begin. A makeshift dais had been set up under the projection screen, with two armchairs and a low table, bottles of water, and microphones. Peter Atkins came in, followed by a bearded man wearing a loden. For each retreat, Peter tried to bring in a specialist in the field addressed by the live challenge. This year, it was Gianfranco Paolini, who worked for the European External Action Service, the diplomatic arm of the EU. He had arrived from Brussels that morning. He removed his loden and took his place on the dais. He was a man of about fifty, salt-and-pepper beard, corduroy suit, checkered shirt, and wine-red tie. Peter had invited him to evaluate the pertinence of our conclusions, as if he were an actual client who had commissioned a forecasting study. After a brief introduction, the first group (Enid Eelmäe's group) took the mic. I knew from Enid that their work hadn't gone well. No one had said a word because one member had monopolized the conversation, a woman who was very reserved at first, even shy, but who, the moment they had gotten started, had become deeply immersed in their discussions and lost all professional objectivity. She had very precise ideas about the question and wouldn't hear otherwise, refusing any sort of dialogue. The group's only options were to agree with her or sit by angrily. Enid confessed that she didn't understand how someone could invest so much emotion in what was basically just role-playing. This woman had really entered into the game, she said. For her, it wasn't a game at all, it was as if her life depended on it. All this to tell us that we were heading straight into the abyss. I know we had the darkest scenario, Enid said, but even so, such an apocalyptic vision! To present its report, Enid Eelmäe's group had designated a very thin woman, dressed entirely in black and with sunken cheeks. The moment she stood up, I guessed it was the woman Enid had told me about. Pythian appearance, pale complexion, long black hair streaked with gray: the woman began reading the paper in her hand, an exalted expression in her eyes. Old Europe with its declining population will be confronted in 2030 with serious energy crises. Pollution resulting from intensive agriculture has reduced the supply of fresh water, which has already become scarce through global warming. The continent's fishing fleets have been inactive since the total depletion of fish stocks in the North Sea. At that moment, the door to the room opened and Scott Adams appeared. He entered without making a sound and did not take a seat, though there were several empty chairs. Instead, he conspicuously went to lean against the wall and crossed his arms, a smug look on his face, listening to the speaker but knowing full well that most eyes were now on him. He had immediately put a pall over the room. I saw Peter Atkins looking somber and annoyed, not knowing whether to get up and ask him to leave or to let him watch the proceedings, even if it meant putting up with his sarcastic remarks and mocking looks for the rest of the meeting. The woman continued to read her relentless indictment into the mic. Technological progress could in no way slow this decline, for technology is but the reflection of the dominant values of the society that produces it. When she finished her expose, she sat back down. There was a general murmur, but no one applauded. Scott Adams smiled slyly. Peter Atkins took the mic and launched into a broad-strokes commentary on what we had just heard, but he was talking in a vacuum. He had difficulty finding his words, was visibly uninspired, his mind seemed elsewhere, his attention entirely taken up by the disturbing presence of Scott Adams in his field of vision. He cut short his remarks and gave the floor to the second group, which had worked on a scenario called "Empire Europe." The group's reporter made a precise, succinct presentation, developing several original ideas that enriched the discussion. The same was true for the third group, for which the spokesperson, a woman with a soft voice, more intellectual and literary, presented a scenario called "Social Communion." The presentations were of a high level, carefully articulated and reasoned. They were the types of reflections that could have been generated by the best think tanks, which have always been particularly effective in the realm of international politics. But what I found troubling about this exercise was that, even though the participants gave very cogent and well-structured reports, even though you could sense their acumen and subtle intuition, in the final account they were built on thin air. For in reality, we had no real assessment indicators at our disposal to gauge the topics we had been asked to study, and even if we had had all the available data, our choices, the decisions we might have suggested, didn't have and would never have any impact on real life. The people around me were used to pondering such matters, they knew how to analyze and structure their thoughts. They seemed to know the topic well, and presented their findings rationally, clearly, and coherently. But in reality, it was only a phantom—a situation that, it occurred to me, was not unlike the one in which politicians found themselves on a daily basis.

The spokesperson for the third group was discussing Brexit, and I thought with bitter irony that, even though the Brexit hypothesis had cropped up occasionally in forecasting scenarios over the past months, now that the results of the British referendum were known, no one had bothered checking those old forecasts to see what had been predicted. It was as if the forecasting scenarios we elaborated so carefully were valid only when articulated, and that, as soon as the reality of the situation put our conclusions to the test, we immediately moved on to something else, imagined new scenarios for yet another future. I feared we were eternally running in place like a hamster in its wheel, eyes permanently fixed on a distant horizon. This was one of the recurrent Achilles' heels of futurology, that the recommendations we made never, or so rarely, panned out in real life. However brilliant our analyses, however perceptive our intuitions, their articulation remained slack, the driving belt defective, between the conclusions we reached and the decisions actually made by political leaders. For politicians are rarely inclined to take a long view in their decision-making, for the simple reason that responses to future demands would take effect only much later (if ever), when the people implementing them were no longer in office. What good is it to make difficult and unpopular decisions if they can't help you win the next election? This was particularly striking today in the sphere of climate change, where the most elementary and urgent measures were constantly being deferred.

When the spokesperson for the third group had finished her presentation, Scott Adams raised his hand to ask a question. A chill settled over the room, an invisible heightening of tension in the air. Scott Adams kept his hand raised, a trace of insolent smile on his lips. Peter looked at him, unsure how to react. The silence dragged on, and it was as if the two men were engaging in a symbolic arm wrestle. The EU representative, on the dais, looked unsettled by the scene. I could see his glance darting back and forth between this unknown person with his hand raised—who, as far as he was concerned, should be allowed to speak—and Peter, rigid on his chair, glaring balefully at Scott Adams. Finally, in a glacial voice, he said that, for the purposes of methodology—and he stressed the word *methodology*, knowing that this was purportedly Scott Adams's field of expertise—he preferred that all questions wait until after the presentations. Scott Adams remained frozen for a moment, hand still raised, then slowly let it drop, as if putting a gun back in its holster. Then he snickered more loudly, and taking the room as witness: "You see what I mean, you can't even ask a question here," and Gianfranco Paolini seemed increasingly dumbstruck at the scene playing out before his eyes—when, all of a sudden, Scott Adams strode quickly toward the dais. I glimpsed Gianfranco Paolini's and Peter's horrified faces as they watched him take determined steps toward them. Scott Adams stopped directly in front of Peter, who jerked back in his chair, and said, mere inches from his face: "Very well, I'll ask my question later." Then, spinning on his heel, he left the room, slamming the door behind him.

Peter Atkins took a gulp of water, hands slightly shaking. He picked up the mic but mixed up his pages and instead passed the floor to our group. Scott Adams's violent exit had cast a pall over the room. Everyone's mind was elsewhere as Carmen Zúñiga and Viswanathan Ajit Pai reported our findings. I noticed several private conversations being held at the other tables (on the dais, Peter was leaning toward Gianfranco Paolini and murmuring something). Once our group's report was over, Gianfranco Paolini took the mic. He began by thanking us for the high quality of our presentations. He didn't wish, and didn't consider it his place, to review each scenario in detail. He remained very diplomatic, not mentioning assertions he'd found unconvincing, and said he was looking forward to reading the final document we'd be producing. Of course, this was merely an exercise, but he was certain that our analyses could help nourish discussions about new foreign policies in the EU. Two points in particular had caught his attention. The first was that we had underscored, rightly, that Europe's capacity for innovation was not sufficiently employed as a strategic resource in foreign relations. The second point concerned the politics of migration. In that regard, our idea to use immigrants already residing in Europe as a resource, by dealing with them directly and not going through their governments, was in his view an extremely fruitful one. Viswanathan quietly stood up as Gianfranco Paolini was speaking and crept around the table, crouching low, to give Carmen Zúñiga a goodbye hug. He shook my hand, went to retrieve his rolling suitcase against the wall, and discreetly left the room. A cab had been called and was waiting for him in the courtyard of Hartwell House. He had a dinner in London that evening and would be flying to Asia in the morning. Viswanathan was always between two trains or two planes. When he drafted a report, he was already thinking of the next telephone call, and when he was on that call, he was thinking of the meeting he was to attend immediately afterward. He must have been in his taxi by now, heading toward Aylesbury station, and lord knows what messages he was tapping into his phone.

When I came down from my room for the gala dinner that evening, it hit me again that this was my last night in Hartwell House, and that I'd be leaving for Brussels the next morning. Drinks had been served in the library. I looked around for Enid Eelmäe, but she hadn't yet arrived.

I downed a glass of champagne and joined in several random conversations. I went over to Peter, who confided that he was very bitter about the way the retreat had gone this year. He couldn't go into any detail, as there were too many people around, but he told me in a murmur that he had feared from the start that Scott Adams would be trouble. Still, he never would have imagined how unpleasant and contentious the man could be, would never have thought that Adams would go out of his way to sabotage the proceedings so badly and end up making such a scene. Some great idea of mine to invite him, he said with a mischievous twinkle, and he began to laugh, glass in hand, with that particular laugh of his (even in French, his laugh had an English accent). After leaving Peter to his regrets, I went to refill my glass of champagne. I still hadn't spotted Enid. Even though we hadn't been in the same work group during the retreat, we had spent most of the week together. We met up during breaks and ate at the same table. Several times, after dinner, we would go for a walk in the park. Viswanathan Ajit Pai had noticed our closeness, but had shown discretion, even tact, and had delicately moved aside to let her join me when he'd seen her appear in the doorway one day during a coffee break. Cocktail hour was almost over, and some people were already heading into the dining room. I followed them, hesitantly. A large gala table had been set up, decorated with flowers and candles: white tablecloth, silver tableware, and an assortment of crystal glasses that sparkled beneath the lit chandeliers. I didn't take my seat immediately. I went over to the terrace doors, watched the rain in the park through the glass panes. Night hadn't yet fallen, but the rain was drenching the lawns. Enid still hadn't showed, and I finally went to sit at the end of the table, where a few empty places remained. A dozen or so people were still missing, polishing off one last aperitif in the library or still up in their rooms. I kept throwing furtive glances at the doorway, and finally I saw Enid come in, wearing an elegant black dress. She came up and took a seat next to me, smiling and touching my arm to apologize for her delay.

As soon as Enid was beside me, I felt a wave of relief. I felt safe near her, protected by her aura, sheltered in the cocoon of our conversation that isolated us from the outside world and the other diners, as if inside a glass bubble. We chatted for ourselves alone, about topics amusing and frivolous, heedless of the voices around us. We had spent a lot of time together since the beginning of the retreat but had rarely touched on personal matters, such as whether or not we were married, or if we had children. We had remained evasive about private details. I had thought we might take a last walk in the park that evening, but the rain made it impossible, and I experienced a keen disappointment. I had already drunk a fair amount of wine at dinner, and I took my glass with me when I got up from the table. As it was our last evening, many of the attendees had migrated to the bar. There were people in every room, talking in the salons; the atmosphere was celebratory. A colleague of Linda Smith's, who worked with her at the Pentagon, was among the most exuberant. He had joined the little group formed by Enid, Linda Smith, and me, and had latched onto our conversation. Taking us by the shoulders, he gathered the three of us under his wings and dragged us to the bar, with the intention of making us sample every bourbon on the menu, Jefferson's, Jim Beam, Four Roses, Wild Turkey. The evening stretched on, conversations intermingled, new groups formed. Enid and I retreated into the library, where three or four others, among them Gianfranco Paolini, were having a drink, deep into a studious and professional discussion. We went to sit some distance away. The group ended up leaving and we found ourselves alone. The library was warm, wood-paneled, with hundreds of books aligned on shelves protected by fine metal mesh. I got up to fetch two more drinks at the bar and, when I returned, instead of sitting opposite Enid on the armchair, I sat next to her on the sofa. I had stayed with whiskey, and Enid had preferred to return to white wine after the syrupy interlacing of bourbons (of which, moreover, she had taken only a few reluctant sips). I handed her her wine and we toasted, quietly, gazing into each other's eyes. I felt frozen, intimidated. I wanted to put my hand on her arm, but I didn't dare make a move. There is always a moment, in love relations, when, even if you know your bodies will end up coming together, that you will be embracing, that a kiss is imminent, you remain in expectancy, and nothing will happen if you don't decide to act. Even if both of you know that something intimate is liable to occur at any moment, there is one last river to cross, which you might realize in retrospect was just a tiny stream, easily forded, but which, as long as you haven't waded across it, remains an insurmountable obstacle. There is always that last symbolic threshold between pleasurable anticipation and the expected outcome of hand finding hand and lips finding lips. And perhaps it's because the anticipation is often so pleasurable that, for my part, I've rarely gone further. As if it was in the bliss of promise that I had lived my most wonderful hours of love. There is an adage in chess that says that threat is stronger than execution, and I had the feeling that if I modified this slightly, replaced "threat" with "promise" and "execution" with "realization," this adage could apply just as well to love. I looked at Enid and discerned clear signs of loving complicity in the calm smiles and confident gazes we continued to share on the sofa—such that I was all the more staggered by what happened next. At one moment, Enid stood up and, not knowing what she was doing or intended to do, I stood up after her, and we found ourselves standing face-to-face in the library. She moved closer to me, slowly, and put her hand on my shoulder. With a very tender, very emotional look in her eyes, she kissed me on the cheek and said it had been a great pleasure to know me and spend the week together. Then she walked away, gave me another wave from a distance, and left the room—and I didn't see her again (the next day, when I came down for breakfast, she was already gone).

I sat back down on the sofa, utterly dejected, a great emptiness in my chest. I remained that way for ten minutes, alone in the library, at what must have been past two in the morning. I finished my glass of whiskey and decided to go have another. There was almost no one left in the hotel, a couple in one of the salons, a young woman sitting alone at the bar. I asked the bartender for a bourbon. While he poured, I asked the young woman if I could offer her a drink. A margarita, she said. It wasn't the first time I'd seen her. She wasn't quite a participant in the retreat, but she seemed to be connected with it; I think she had assisted Peter Atkins with the organization. She confirmed this, saying she was the retreat coordinator. I didn't really know what "coordinator" meant, and in any case I didn't care, had no desire to talk about work, so rather than asking her what, exactly, a coordinator was, I asked her what, exactly, a margarita was. It's a tequila cocktail, she said, and the bartender, who was mixing it in the shaker, joined in to list the ingredients: tequila, Cointreau, lime juice. When the bartender ceremoniously deposited the margarita in front of the woman, she picked up the glass with its lacing of salt and raised it toward me in thanks. The cocktail looked delicious. Perhaps she guessed what I was thinking, as she asked if I wanted to try a sip. I nodded and, sliding down the bar to join her, I climbed onto the adjacent stool. She handed me her glass and I dipped my lips in it. So? I nodded again. It was very refreshing, and I signaled to the bartender to make me one too. Sitting at the bar next to the young woman, I continued with her the conversation I'd begun with Enid in the library. It wasn't exactly the same conversation, even supposing we could have recreated the exact topic of the exquisite and meandering conversation I'd been having with Enid, but it had the same tone, the same way of talking, at once serious, lighthearted, and in league, punctuated by half smiles and insistent gazes. Sitting side by side at the bar, our hands brushed, and I kept talking to her as if all the conversations I'd had with Enid since the beginning of the week had been with her instead. In short, I acted with her as if we already shared a long and tender understanding, which gave my movements a certain ease and my words assurance. Glass in hand, I leaned toward her shoulder and whispered in her ear an allusion to a conversation we'd had at dinner, as if I didn't realize that it was not Enid at my side. It is often like that in life, when one's way of being with a woman one has just met, the conversations one can have with her (and later, who knows, the tender attentions and caresses, and even subsequent quarrels and breakups), complement or complete, correct or amend, the conversations one has had with another woman—as if, in our inveterate solipsism, it was always to one single woman, who subsumes all the women in one's life, that one were speaking. Moreover, it wasn't impossible that the young woman had herself begun the evening with another man, and that she was pursuing with me an amorous banter initiated with someone else, so that, in speaking to me, she was talking to someone beyond myself, someone who also included the stranger with whom she'd spent the early hours of the evening. The traces of our past loves are not yet erased when new imprints, marks of burgeoning affairs, come to add to them, superimpose themselves and blend with them. I had no idea what time it might be—three, four in the morning. Who knows how much longer we would have stayed in that bar if the bartender, noticing that there was no one else left, hadn't announced that he was about to close. He asked if we'd like one last drink, and I signaled to him to make us two more margaritas (I don't know how many of them we'd downed by this point). The bartender finished putting away his utensils behind the counter. He turned off the lights and we left the room, crossed the silent lobby of the hotel in the dark, and started together up the majestic staircase of Hartwell House.

The next day, putting my hand in my jacket pocket, I felt an unusual item under my fingers: a cigarette, a menthol filter cigarette, whole, white, intact. I had no memory of that cigarette, even if I knew where it had likely come from. I could easily imagine that the young woman had offered me one at some point the previous evening, and that, even though I didn't smoke, for fun or seduction, to affirm our closeness, I had taken it. I must have toyed with that cigarette between my fingers, perhaps even put it to my lips, though obviously hadn't smoked it. But since I had no memory of that cigarette or of how it had ended up there—none whatsoever—I could also imagine that other things, less insignificant, less harmless, more intimate, had also occurred between us. I tried several times after that to recall exactly what had happened that night with that woman. I started with the few facts I had in my possession and tried to move farther back in time to reconstruct the evening's events. One thing I hazily remembered was that we had paused on the second-floor landing after leaving the bar. We had stopped next to the railing, uncertain, not knowing whether to prolong the evening, in my room or hers, when she had said—and I remember perfectly the intonation of her words in English: "Let's go to my place" (what struck me was that she hadn't said *to my room*, but *to my place*), and, stumbling on the carpet, we had started down a long, empty hallway toward her room at four in the morning. After that, my memory gets foggy, a black hole, a kind of amnesia due to too much alcohol. Entire portions of the evening remain inaccessible, as if they had been erased forever. The image that then comes back to me is of her in that hotel room, walking back and forth in front of me in the semi-dark, a single bedside lamp diffusing a muted light. She is barefoot, her white blouse is half-undone, she is wearing elegant black trousers of lightweight silk that flare and undulate up and down her legs. That's all. Try as I might to recall what happened after that, there's nothing, only haze. And suddenly it came back to me, the entire scene came back to me. I'm standing facing her in the half-dark, when, for fun, for a lark, I pull my phone from my pocket and take her picture. She is lying back in front of me in the large yellow armchair with frills, having removed her blouse and in only her bra. She smiles at me, with no trace of shyness. She strikes different poses, spreads her arms, lets her head fall back and loosens her hair. I talk to her, we banter, and suddenly she removes her bra, which she sets down languidly, arm outstretched, next to her on the carpet. There is a challenge in her eyes. She looks at me. With breasts bared, she offers herself to me. I raise my phone and see her half-naked body in the viewer—and I take the picture. And it's that photo that was still in my phone, that photo that I had never deleted. I'm not entirely sure what happened after that. The only thing I know for certain is that I did not spend the night with her, that I awoke alone in my room in Hartwell House the next morning.

II

MY FATHER DIED IN DECEMBER OF THAT same year, 2016. I learned of his passing on my return from a trip to Asia. I cut short the trip to be at his bedside as soon as I heard his health had deteriorated, but I wasn't fast enough to see him once more, as he was already gone when I arrived. If I had gotten there in time, would I have found him awake in his bed? Could I have told him, as I imagined it during the flight home, that I had thought of him while pondering the golden ginkgo leaves covering the timeless pathways of the University of Tokyo? Would he have said anything to me, a sentence that would have stayed forever in my memory as his last words? I don't know. The scene never took place, and maybe it's better that way.

The day of my father's funeral, we held a vigil for his body in his study until it was time to leave for La Cambre Abbey, where the service was to be held. The drapes were half-drawn, and a discreet twilight enveloped the room. I was standing by the French doors, looking in silence at the back garden of my parents' house, the gravel path with its rosebushes bending under the rain in the December gray. I was alone in the room with Pierre, my brother. Pierre didn't look much like me, even if an expert eye could have spotted minute similarities between us. We no doubt had a family resemblance, but it was almost impossible to detect. Physically, Pierre took after my father, while I took after my mother. And even those resemblances weren't obvious, not blatant as in certain families, in which the parents seem to have engendered reduced carbon copies of themselves, miniature clones posing next to them in family photos. No, the resemblances between us, if they existed, were much more obscure, almost clandestine, subtly interwoven, each of us having mixed a pinch of resemblance from the other parent in with the primary resemblance. But in attitude, and more generally in temperament, as well as in our choice of professions, Pierre the architect was incontestably De Groef, and I was mainly Detrez like my father, a diplomat and university professor who had served as a European commissioner, and in whose footsteps I'd followed by also joining the European Commission.

Pierre and I shared a certain number of references all our own, a kind of private language composed of words and idiomatic expressions that established a secret bond between us. Most of this repertoire would have left others indifferent, but for us it took on a particularly intimate meaning, which made our ears perk up when one of those terms cropped up by chance in conversation. It might be a simple adjective, like "redhibitory," which seemed to belong not to common vocabulary but rather to my father's personal lexicon, as if he were the only one ever to have used the word. It signified that a thing or situation had a radical constituent flaw that made it unacceptable, and whenever I heard the word *redhibitory* in conversation, I couldn't help thinking of my father and feeling a wave of nostalgia. It might also be an expression that evoked something specific for us, and only for us. This was the case with the expression "the revenge of the Kroumir," which my father was particularly fond of (the origin and etymology of *Kroumir* long remained a mystery). And how many times, in our adolescence, did my brother and I hear my father use the expression "Where did you put the nail clippers?"—as if, in the apartment we occupied on Rue Saint-Guillaume in Paris in the 1970s, there had been only one pair of nail clippers, a single, precious nail clipper (unfindable, by definition). For to my father's paranoid mind, and God knows why, his two sons, with their mother's connivance, were constantly engaged in hiding the family's one pair of nail clippers, intentionally misplacing and concealing it. And, rather than simply buy another pair (which, once I'd reached adulthood, I lost no time in doing, compulsively hoarding nail clippers during my two successive marriages, stockpiling them like a squirrel with its nuts to compensate for the slight residual adolescent trauma), my father would burst from the bathroom, bare-chested and with a towel wrapped around his loins, and, shaking with rage, ransack the house for his nail clippers, making the walls of the Rue Saint-Guillaume apartment shake as he yelled down the hall, "Where the hell are the goddam nail clippers! What have you done now with the nail clippers!?" Every family must have its totem, talismanic, or taboo words, which exceed their simple meaning to take on a mythological dimension; words that contain an amplified, and no doubt irrational, emotional resonance that exasperate us as teenagers, but that later, with age and the deaths of the protagonists, become poignant, that we happen upon through life's vicissitudes with pure tenderness—as if, the further childhood and adolescence recede into the past, the more our memory tints each tiny facet of it in rose.

I'm three years older than Pierre, but I've always felt as if he were the older sibling. Moreover, I think that, unconsciously, he always wanted to convey the sense that he was my big brother. I have several objective reasons for thinking this, as Pierre established himself socially very early on, or in any case well before me. At age twenty-six, he was already running his own architectural firm: when our grandfather De Groef died in 1989, he was the one who took over De Groef Architects. Our family had lived in Paris since the early 1970s, after my father had been appointed to UNESCO. Pierre was barely out of architecture school, and my mother, who had no intention of leaving Paris to take over her father's business (she enjoyed her full-time occupation as her husband's éminence grise), encouraged Pierre to move to Brussels. Pierre familiarized himself with Belgian legislation, saw to all the paperwork, bought out my mother's and my shares, and become sole proprietor of the De Groef firm, which he rebaptized DG&D Architects—for De Groef and Detrez—and which he has now run for the past thirty years.

Pierre had always wanted to be an architect. His path seemed to have been determined from the get-go, from even before he was born. My mother, by naming him after her own grandfather, the architect Pierre De Groef, had more or less marked him as a De Groef and tacitly enjoined him to become an architect himself. Our parents' invisible choices, their secret, subliminal desires, often guide our lives much more than we realize. As with many people who, from earliest childhood, are fated to practice the same profession as their parents or grandparents, who have decided that they will take over the family concern (whether notarial practice, vineyard, or architectural office), Pierre took up the torch that several generations of De Groefs had passed down to him and became the brilliant architect that my mother privately dreamed of him becoming. But while our great-grandfather Pierre De Groef, whom we hadn't known, and on whose knees my mother herself had barely had time to bounce (he died when she was six), was doubtless an honorable and respectable ancestor, he was not the most inspiring model for the idealistic young architect my brother was in the early 1980s. There was a hiccup. The hiccup, the sore point, was that, as my mother one day summed it up: "My grandfather despised Horta."

Having in our ancestry an architect who had practiced in Brussels at the time of the great Art Nouveau revolution seemed less exciting once we realized that he was only a neoclassical bourgeois, who adopted various styles and loved Louis XV furniture. My brother and I, snobs that we were (especially my brother the architecture student), figured that if we were to have an architect for a great-grandfather, we wanted it to be Victor Horta himself! Still, as we grew older, we came to realize that there was nothing shameful in descending from Pierre De Groef, a virtuoso of the Beaux-Arts style, who enjoyed plenty of success in his day despite the frenzy for Art Nouveau. It's true that

Horta was a visionary, who conceived of architecture as a global, all-encompassing phenomenon, as one can see from the many refinements in his studio on Rue Américaine, from the floor mosaics to the cast-iron volutes of the staircase ramps. (For his clients, Horta would go so far as to design the owner's gown.) Horta made history; our great-grandfather was content to do his job. The first years of the twentieth century were a lively and dynamic period for architecture in Brussels. There were debates, schools, tendencies. An emerging urban bourgeoisie wanted private houses, and the most enlightened of them tried to stand out by making bold statements: it was they, the Autriques and the Tassels, who went to Victor Horta. But there was also a more conventional middle class that preferred to hire our great-grandfather, who was no innovator but who, working in classical fashion with handsome materials, created comfortable houses, notably incorporating modern conveniences like central heating or private elevators. In less than twenty years, Pierre De Groef, who hailed from a modest background (his father was a cabinetmaker from Ixelles), had become a fashionable architect, a well-to-do citizen, an established bourgeois: mustache, flannel suit with vest and watch fob, and wide polka-dot tie, as he appears on the photo that for many years embellished the kitchen of my parents' home on Avenue Emile Duray. At the time, the Ixelles Ponds area, on which he'd set his sights, was still mostly rural. He was smart enough to buy up all the plots of land surrounding La Cambre Abbey, which was being restored after the First World War. He then made it a condition for anyone buying the plots he owned that he would be the architect of anything built on it. And so he built six houses on Avenue des Klauwaerts and as many on Avenue Emile Duray, including the apartment at number 28 that my parents rented once they returned from Paris at the end of the 1990s.

It was Pierre De Groef's son, Marcel, my maternal grandfather, who took over the practice upon his father's death. Marcel De Groef thus found himself at the peak of his professional activity in Brussels in the early 1950s, a period of intense architectural effervescence. It was the end of the Second World War and the beginning of modernism, whose apogee would be the Universal Exposition of 1958, when entire neighborhoods of Brussels were razed. They demolished dozens of old houses to build skyscrapers and offices. They dug tunnels and widened the roadways into outsized boulevards. They disfigured Avenue Louise by making it into a "vehicular access point," the inelegance of the expression equaled only by the brutality of the profanation. Sidewalks were narrowed, venerable chestnut trees chopped down. Faced with the commotion of this mammoth construction site, my grandfather, who marched to a different drummer, pursued his activities in a minor mode, continuing to play the piccolo in his quiet corner, while over Brussels crashed the apocalyptic brasses from the finale of a Bruckner symphony. It was the children of his father's clients who now hired the De Groef firm. At the time, transmission was hereditary: you engaged the same suppliers as your parents had. The architect was like the family doctor, with clientele handed down from father to son. My grandfather thus worked for his father's clients' heirs, for whom he designed sturdy houses in the margins left untouched by the demolition and construction fever that was mutilating Brussels. Parallel to his work as a builder, my grandfather took an interest in heritage preservation, even though the term "heritage preservation" didn't yet exist, and the concept even less. The paradox was that, in defending the architectural heritage of Brussels, he would also, perforce, have to defend Horta's constructions against the forces of demolition. A sad witness to the urban massacre perpetrated in the guise of modernization, my grandfather would be helpless to save the Maison du Peuple and would watch in dismay as they quartered and dismembered the façade of the Aubecq Hotel. Against all odds, however, he helped save from ruin several of Horta's masterpieces, the building of which must have enraged his father as a young architect. It was a singular reversal of viewpoint, in which the conservationists of the time should preserve the most avant-garde constructions of the past, and in which, in one family, the son—out of fidelity to his father's preservationist spirit—was led to protect a body of work that the father abhorred. In the same context, at the end of the 1960s, my grandfather found himself in categorical opposition to a truculent individual whose flinty, metallic name echoed through my childhood: Paul Vanden Boeynants, alderman of Brussels and several times minister, a politician and a butcher, with a Brussels accent you could cut with a knife (no doubt a butcher knife), known by his initials, VDB, which some local wags had transformed into Veal de Beef. And while my heart, or my discernment (in a reconstituted memory that I've perhaps embellished to flatter my Europeanness), holds up Paul-Henri Spaak as the most significant political figure of my childhood years, in my gut I mainly remember Paul Vanden Boeynants.

As a child, Pierre was constantly telling Grandpa Marcel that he was going to be an architect just like him, and I think that my grandfather took pleasure in seeing himself so warmly cosseted in the family history between his own father and this grandson who was set on perpetuating the De Groef architectural line. While my grandfather never expressed this pleasure aloud (other than in the amused encouragements he gave the little boy who drew houses in crayon, or the sage advice that, toward the end of his life, he lavished on the young architecture student in Paris), he must have been flattered by the promise that his legacy would be carried forward by his descendants. It was no doubt a similar pleasure that my father would have felt had he been able to witness the scene we were living that morning in his study; had he been able to see, from the place where he was now, the immaterial place from which he continued to haunt our consciousness, his two adult sons standing around his casket. We put on our coats and left the house to go to La Cambre Abbey, and I'm not sure why, but the image of two adult sons in suits and ties and dark overcoats around their father's casket is the one I'd later retain of that day. Perhaps because it was the first time I glimpsed what my own funeral might be like, with my own children, having by then become adults, standing around *my* casket in dark overcoats: Alessandro, my eldest son, in a belted wool coat with a black velvet collar, the big brother protectively surrounding his younger brother, Thomas, and sister, Tessa, my nine-year-old twins. Tessa, my little girl transformed into a grown woman, following my coffin wearing dark glasses, head lowered, mouth hidden behind a gray woolen scarf. And the image of adult children around their father's casket, rather than horrifying me or seeming morbid, instead struck me as peaceful, in that it seemed to participate in the natural order of things. In my heart of hearts, at that painful moment in my father's study, it afforded me a measure of comfort.

As an architect, Pierre had enjoyed a dizzying ascent. Promoting the notion of durable architecture from as far back as his student days—in this regard, he was ahead of the curve—he had built himself a sophisticated private clientele in Europe, as well as in Asia, where his work had always found favor. The graft had taken between the contemporary concern for durable construction and old know-how, the tradition of the De Groef architectural office. Like his grandfather and great-grandfather before him, Pierre had become an architect for his own time, respectful of environmental regulations, favoring materials with strong thermal inertia for framing and roofing, and finding innovative ecological solutions for insulation, such as wadding, cellulose, and plant fibers. His big break came in 1996, when he was chosen to renovate the Berlaymont building. After a first round open exclusively to Belgian architects, he ultimately found himself a finalist, opposite internationally renowned figures like Norman Foster and Jean Nouvel. His main advantage was that he again based his project entirely on durable construction. What he proposed was to make the old Berlaymont building from the 1960s—an old admiralty vessel, stodgy, sclerotic, riddled with friable asbestos, and completely energy-inefficient; a shadowy place of Borgesian staircases that led nowhere and confusing overhead gangways like something out of a Piranesi prison—into something bright and transparent. According to the metaphor Pierre had used during his interview with the European Commission, he wanted to transform this big, fat, gas-guzzling American sedan into a little Twingo with a catalytic converter. The expression caught on, and his proposal was chosen by the Berlaymont 2000 company. Pierre was only thirty-two, but Renzo Piano had been scarcely more than thirty when he won the competition for the Pompidou Center, and Dominique Perrault only thirty-six when he was chosen to design the new Bibliothèque Nationale. After that early acme in his career, Pierre continued to develop his thinking, stripping more and more away. Frugal, economical, pushing into minimalism, pursuing an ideal of modesty and constantly seeking to eliminate clutter, he invented the concept of *interstitial architecture*. He became interested in exiguous models and minuscule spaces, in the air or underground, small-dimension parcels squeezed between two structures or located between two existing houses; an XXS form of architecture whose ambition was to reconnect with the fundamentals of the discipline: space, which he would emphasize rather than fill, and light, which he'd spread. Fascinated by Japan, and more recently by China, Pierre one day reflected to me: "Throughout his life, the Westerner piles up and accumulates, whereas the Asian lightens and divests himself. When death comes, the Asian has only a purified, unburdened body to offer death, whereas the Westerner dies surrounded by his *brols*!" (And that final Belgicism, with which he had spiced his punchline, was accompanied by a gleam in his eye of jocular kinship.) These past years, Pierre had been working on ever more limited spaces, which sometimes didn't exceed nine cubic meters, like his latest creation in Tokyo: a cantilevered glass die floating in the sky, extending from a glass footbridge on the eighteenth floor of a building in Harajuku. (I can only imagine the face on Grandpa Marcel if he'd seen his grandson's blueprints for it!)

In 1998 or 1999, I don't remember which, Pierre arranged for my father and me to visit the Berlaymont construction site. I was still living in Paris at the time and had gone to Brussels to spend the weekend with my parents. My father wasn't yet at the European Commission, but my parents had returned to live in Brussels a year or two earlier, my father having taken on some duties with the Institute of European Studies. It was overcast on the day of the visit, one of those humid days when it never stops raining. My father watched for our taxi through the bay window of the living room on Avenue Emile Duray. He was ready to go, having already put on his coat and gloves and carefully knotted his scarf around his neck. He kept compulsively checking his watch, then cast more glances through the window. He looked nervous. He was always nervous when he had to go out or change locations, when taking a train or an airplane or even just walking into a restaurant. Perhaps that worry was secretly related to the fear of death, that rite of passage that we all have to go through someday, and that had now happened for my father, for all eternity. It was always in transitional moments that his disquiet appeared so acutely, in life's interstices, moments of suture or articulation, hinge moments—I know this from experience, as I have the same disquiet. Then, once the critical moment was over, once he was settled in his train or plane, the anxiety would pass, and my father would relax and become the most charming of men. That day, as I recall, the taxi didn't show, even though my father had given himself plenty of time and called the company he habitually used, Taxis Verts. We had been preparing for this visit for weeks, including filling out an information sheet and making copies of our passports; we had even undergone a physical exam because of the potential hazards from asbestos exposure on the site. We'd then sent all the documentation to Pierre, who had gotten us special access passes. And now, because the taxi hadn't come, we were liable to miss it, and my father was beside himself. When he finally did call the cab company, he got a rather uncooperative dispatcher and, tense, angry, with cold fury in his eyes, my father exploded on the telephone, his natural worry having mutated into a wave of irrational angst at the prospect of being late. And so our departure from Avenue Emile Duray was anything but smooth. I don't recall why my mother wasn't with us that day, but no doubt it was for the best, as my mother's presence usually aggravated my father's anxiety. All they would have needed was a minor disagreement over some insignificant point (points of minor disagreement were not lacking between them), and my mother's observations would have further irritated my father. My parents often had interminable arguments, not to say truly Byzantine rhetorical jousts. They were both formidable debaters (my mother more of a sophist, my father more combative); if the argument started as we left the house, it would continue throughout the taxi ride. My mother never let go a point of view, never let a position drop, never gave up about anything. My father, already agitated and anxious, would work himself into an uncontrollable rage, which, under my mother's incessant needling and ostensibly innocent teasing, put him in an absolute state, which usually ended in a screaming fight—as I often witnessed when I came to visit them.

Having finally showed up, the taxi let us off at the Robert Schuman Roundabout. I left my father to pay the fare and got out of the car under the driving rain. I raised my eyes toward the construction site, immediately captivated by the tall cranes, their jibs creaking and shaking in the wind and rain. Standing on the sidewalk, I looked up at the Berlaymont—the Berlaymont!—and I realized that this huge building rising before my eyes, this building whose aura surpassed its physical materiality, this world-renowned building that embodied the symbolic value of European institutions—I realized that I was truly seeing it for the first time. Of course, I had always been familiar with it: it was located only a few miles as the crow flies from the house where I'd spent my childhood, and it had been built when I was living in Brussels (though I was too young to remember its construction, and even if I had known that they were building the future seat of the European Commission, it would have meant nothing to me at the time). But, odd as it seemed, I didn't recall ever having been this close to the Berlaymont. I was standing on the sidewalk, gazing at the imposing structure that soared up under the rain. I could make out its shape, sense its presence on the edges of the

Schuman Roundabout. It was the first time I was truly seeing it, though in fact I couldn't really see it at all, as it was entirely hidden under a vast white construction tarpaulin streaming with rainwater.

My father joined me, and we looked around for Pierre, but there was no sign of him. We headed off under the pelting rain, raising the collars of our coats, skirting the hermetically sealed area of the site with its surrounding fence. Pierre finally appeared, breathless and annoyed; he was soaked, asked where we'd been, had been waiting for us on Rue de la Loi since our rendezvous time. I explained our problem with the taxi, while my father, a dark look on his face, said nothing, mortified at being late (which he wasn't used to). Not wanting to linger in the downpour, we quickened our steps to a doorway cut into the fencing, where Pierre made us enter, showing a guard his ID and the badges he'd gotten us. We stepped into a no-man's-land under the open sky, following a plank path over the muddy ground. A prefab office stood out in the gray, with a yellow light in the window. Inside, two guys lazing in front of a monitor watched us enter. They examined our passes and gave each of us a pair of boots and coveralls, motioning us toward a bench and coatrack where we could change. I had expected that some precautions would be required to enter the construction zone, but I never imagined they'd be so draconian. I removed my coat, hung it on a peg, and put on the coveralls over my suit. I watched my father struggling with the garment. I don't know how he'd managed it, but the coverall reached only to his waist, and he couldn't grab hold of the top part, which hung down behind him. Pierre, more accustomed to the contortions of putting on coveralls, was already suited up. He had pulled the hood over his head, and he helped my father adjust his protective gear around his shoulders. We put on our safety boots and gloves and were about to enter the site when the two guys from the front handed us masks, with respirators that filtered out asbestos fibers. We adjusted them on our faces with difficulty, then left the prefab office, exiting the decontamination airlock with barely a centimeter of skin exposed. We passed through a second tarpaulin and onto the site, our steps halting, wobbling on the ground like cosmonauts in our thick safety boots. Pierre explained that removing the asbestos from the Berlaymont had been no small feat. They'd first had to take down all the masonry walls, drop ceilings, and anything else liable to contain asbestos. Then, once all that remained of the original building was its skeleton, came the active phase of decontamination. They had first tried using power heaters and blowtorches, but they soon realized that it was causing damage to the steel infrastructure, so they'd had to find another method. Ultimately, the only way to remove the asbestos was by scraping it with a trowel, inch by inch. Pierre brought us to the second floor, and we crossed through a gallery with a low ceiling, where dozens of masked workmen were laboring to extract the asbestos in the semi-darkness, like postapocalyptic shadows. Some, wearing huge goggles, were using portable vacuums that they manipulated at arm's length; others rubbed down the walls with damp cloths. Everywhere, workers in coveralls were scraping the walls to gather up the last residues. Pierre, his mask over his face, treaded carefully in front of us, turning around now and again to say something, his muffled voice reaching us through his respirator. He told us that more than a thousand tons of asbestos had already been removed from the building, and, hearing his cavernous voice come through his mask, which mixed with his breathing in dull asthmatic puffs, it was as if Darth Vader himself were giving us a tour. He added, in his sepulchral, asphyxiated voice, that by certain estimates, with all the asbestos that had been removed from the Berlaymont, the entire building had risen half a foot. As we left the site, following the regulated safety procedures, we were instructed to shower ourselves down. A makeshift decontamination unit had been set up outside, not unlike a car wash, with rows of shower heads on the ceiling that emitted high-pressure jets of soapy water. Skidding over the mud, we went under the showers still dressed in our protective outfits. The rain was coming down, and we showered in the deluge; we could see the rain bouncing off the puddles of water stagnating nearby. Our bodies drenched in soapy water, we vigorously rubbed down our arms and legs with brushes to get the last toxic residues off our coveralls, as if after a chemical attack.

We paid a second visit to the Berlaymont construction site a year or two later, at the beginning of the 2000s. As much as my father, during the first visit, had been withdrawn, so during the second he heavily imposed his presence. Since that first time, he had become a European commissioner, and now he showed up as master of the domain: it was no longer my brother Pierre Detrez showing his family around, but the European commissioner Jean-Yves Detrez who had come to see how the work was progressing, accompanied by his two sons. My father completely overshadowed Pierre (though this would eventually be reversed); his discretion of the first visit was just a distant memory. In his blue cashmere English coat, with his rubber boots and hardhat, he looked like the silent partner, the owner come to inspect the site with his architect, whom he occasionally asked for details about some future development. Pierre and I leaned in eagerly, staying by his side, listening attentively, as he continued through the galleries, hands behind his back, nodding with an earnest air and listening to Pierre's explanations like a chief of state on an official visit. There were now more than a thousand workers on the site, and everywhere people were moving about in a tumult of noise and dust. The original ground floor had been razed, they had relocated the central core, and the thick layers of reinforced concrete that composed it had been recut to clarify the sightlines. A hellish din reigned in the spaces we walked through, as workers attacked the reinforced concrete with jackhammers, which created a phenomenal echo and made the masonry shake. Pierre halted under a girder to give us a glimpse of the planned layout. He was explaining that the spot we were standing on would eventually be the cafeteria, when my father, who'd been nodding impatiently, vaguely annoyed, cut him off to ask where the commissioners' conference room would be located. I could never get used to my father's tendency to always make everything about him. Pierre offered to show him, and we took a construction elevator that rose slowly the length of the façade. At the thirteenth floor, Pierre led us to a vast, grayish space bristling with concrete pillars. The outside air rushed into the site from all sides through huge gaps overlooking the void. The floor was filthy, dusty, smeared with mud and dried cement. We followed Pierre onto a large, bare concrete slab. Here it is, he said, coming to a stop. The commissioners' conference room will be here. My father, in his hardhat and caked boots, stopped next to a wheelbarrow. With a pensive air, he asked where the interpreters' booths would be. Pierre, with a circular movement of his arm, indicated the future booths along the perimeter. My father took a few steps toward what was now just a bare concrete slab, but which one day, lit and lined in blond wood, would be the Jean Monnet Room. I watched him from a distance. He must already have been imagining himself seated beside his colleagues at the large oval conference table. Swarming through his mind must have been sweet visions of remarks made and applauded. With a distant gaze, he seemed elsewhere, lost in his fantasies, and at that moment I was embarrassed to realize just how vain he looked.

My father had irritated me during that visit, and he must have irritated Pierre even more, not being able to help making himself the center of attention, when it was Pierre's project that we had come to see. Perhaps because we were at the Berlaymont, my father had felt obliged to play a role, to don the status of the European commissioner he had become. But who could say whether the vanity he'd let show that day wasn't in fact his normal state? How could we know? Do we always know how our loved ones act when we're not around? Perhaps my father always conducted himself that way in his professional life. I don't believe so, but it's true that we saw him only in a family context. I had kept a low profile during the entire visit, observing my father from outside, coldly, with a critical eye. And it was that same critical eye, which I had inherited from him—for it was he who had given me the weapons I now used to judge him—that had always kept me from being taken in by the comedy of power. I could see perfectly clearly, with the intransigent gaze that I got from him, the futile, vain, illusory nature of the overblown postures that men of influence allowed themselves in public, and what I was witnessing now was my father's own fatuousness. Nonetheless, I couldn't help feeling a pain in my heart thinking back on the scene. In fact, I had felt that affectionate indulgence for my father, the indulgence for our parents' flaws that comes with age, on the very day of our visit to the construction site, and not—or not only—in retrospect.

I didn't know it on the day of that second visit, but paradoxically, the only one of us who would ultimately frequent the Berlaymont with any regularity would be me. If someone had predicted this, none of us would have believed it. Pierre couldn't have known that he would gradually disengage from the project and practically stop setting foot on the site by the time of the building's inauguration—though already, at the time, he was beginning to sense that the adventure was costing him his soul. The project piloted by the Berlaymont 2000 company had become mired in a judicial tussle that had nothing to do with him; financial concerns had ended up overshadowing any esthetic or architectural considerations. And if, as he would later tell me, the main lines of the project as he had conceived of them (especially the new curtain wall with mobile glass screens that he'd envisioned for the façade) would more or less remain, the details he'd specified for the door frames, partitions, woodwork, colors, and materials had all, as he put it, been massacred. My father, who during his visit was already imagining himself presiding at the commissioners' table with such anticipatory delectation, couldn't have known that the project's completion would be several times delayed, and that the Commission that finally took possession of the building, after multiple postponements, would no longer include him. As for me, I would have been the most surprised of all had someone told me that I would frequent the halls of the Berlaymont almost daily, that I would attend numerous meetings there and become a regular of the press room and cafeteria—that less than four years later, *I* would be working for the European Commission.

My father left immediately after the visit; his driver was waiting for him in front of the Berlaymont. I was about to leave as well, but Pierre pulled me aside, wanting to show me the building's foundations. In that spot, below ground, is a truly inextricable knot, he confided, with no fewer than five highway or railroad tunnels passing through it. All five run under the building, or rather they were built *against* the building, meaning that if they'd simply knocked down the original Berlaymont and started fresh, the entire hillside would have collapsed. Come, I'll show you, he said, you'll see, there's a secret passage. Pierre led me into the bowels of the structure. We descended to Level -5, and there, past a heavy fireproof door, he ushered me into a narrow passageway of shadowy concrete lit only by a few green pilot lights. We penetrated into the underground tunnel, and I could feel the symbolic presence of the Berlaymont above our heads, as you can feel the power of the Alps above you if you cross the Gotthard Tunnel on foot. Now and again, Pierre looked back at me with a collusive smile that seemed to stretch across time, as if we were alone in the world, two children on a secret expedition to the center of the Earth. I followed him into the gallery, and we could still hear the construction noise above us. The growl of the jackhammers was sometimes joined by the rumble of a train passing in the distance. Pierre opened a second fire door at the other end of the underground tunnel. We climbed a stairway to reach the surface and suddenly found ourselves back in broad daylight, having emerged farther down the street in the main hall of the Justus Lipsius building. No one batted an eye: it's amazing how few security measures there were at the time. I don't know whether that secret corridor still exists today or whether it has been condemned or destroyed, but ten years later, when I had already been at the European Commission for several years, I would use it to flee the Berlaymont in rather burlesque circumstances.

◆

The day before my father's funeral, after a family dinner on Avenue Emile Duray, I returned home on foot. I was no longer living with Diane and had found myself a studio on Place du Châtelain. It was already dark by the time I left my parents' house. I skirted the Ixelles Ponds. It wasn't very late, not even ten p.m. I walked in the night, thinking about that dinner, where, for the first time, in the large family dining room, we had keenly felt my father's absence.

I followed the path along the ponds, passing by empty benches, shimmering orange lights undulating on the surface of the water. I had known that neighborhood since I was a child. It was also here, five minutes away from my parents', on Rue de Belle-Vue, that Diane and I had found a place in 2007, when the twins were born. How many times had I taken this path to return home after visiting my parents? Coming to the Jardin du Roi, I crossed the street to continue toward Avenue Louise. I had just entered Rue de Belle-Vue when, walking by the building where I had lived with Diane for nearly ten years, I noticed a light in one of our apartment windows. That struck me as odd, as Diane had told me she couldn't attend my father's funeral because she would be leaving Brussels to go on holiday. I had seen her earlier that day, a little past noon, when I'd gone to pick up the twins, and she'd told me she was leaving in just a few hours for winter sports (I didn't know with whom, and didn't care to know). We had exchanged barely a few words in the vestibule, as the twins finished packing their backpacks. I'd found it curious that she'd shown me her plane ticket, pointing to the departure time, 8:40, and the date, as if to prove that she was indeed leaving that night. I had no reason to doubt her, if not for her drawing my attention to something I wouldn't have cared about had she not made such a show of it. I hadn't thought much about it at the time, but it had come back to me later. Wasn't it precisely to exonerate herself, to give me visual proof of her inability to attend my father's funeral, that she had so ostentatiously shown me her ticket? As we parted company, she gave me the requisite condolence peck on the cheek and said to give my mother her love. I thought about this, looking at the light in the fourth-floor window. All the other windows on our floor were dark, and I realized that the light was coming from the small room that Diane had turned into her study. I resumed walking down Rue de Belle-Vue, turning back one last time toward the apartment, when I saw a light go out on the façade. I couldn't immediately tell which light had gone out, as there were several lit windows on other floors of the building. But one light had just gone out, I was sure of it. Could Diane have been in the apartment? Could she have spotted me as I was going by? Could she be watching me, and could she have turned off the light once I'd passed by so that she could observe me without being seen? Was Diane now in the apartment, spying on me in the shadows of the curtains? I retraced my steps but then saw that the light on our floor was still lit; it had stayed the same, that wasn't the light that had gone out. I stopped in front of the building and tried to make out something behind the window. But you couldn't see anything through the window, only the light behind the smoked-glass barrier of the balcony. From where I stood, it was impossible to tell whether any lights were on in other rooms of the apartment, the ones that didn't look out on the street, whether there was anyone, for instance, in the bedroom. I had the key to the apartment in my pocket. I've always kept this key with me, it had been the key to my apartment for almost ten years, and I'd never given it back to Diane. I walked toward the building, passed through the garden gateway, and pushed open the entrance door. I paused a moment before the column of intercom buzzers in the semi-darkness of the glassed-in foyer. I almost buzzed Diane's apartment but thought better of it. I entered the code on the keypad, heard the door click, and went inside. The elevator was on the ground floor; I slipped into the cabin and pushed the button for the fourth floor. I caught my reflection in the mirror, fiddled with the key in my pocket, calmly tense. I looked away, not wanting to see myself just then. The elevator came to a halt and I walked out onto the landing, stopped at our door. How often had I found myself in that exact spot in the past, coming home and sliding the key into the lock without a second thought? Just that afternoon, when I'd come to get the twins, I had been on that landing. I stood motionless in the dark for a moment, alert for any sound. I could hear nothing on the other side of the door. I cautiously slid the key into the lock and opened it. Is anyone home? I called out. I penetrated further into the apartment. Diane? I said. I shut the door behind me. Without turning on the hall light, I headed toward the room where the light was coming from, Diane's study, furnished with a card table supporting stacks of magazines, files, and invoices. I noted that her computer was still there. If she'd gone skiing, why hadn't she taken her laptop with her? I left the room, went down the hall, and stuck my head in the twins' room. It was neat, with nothing lying about on the floor or on the bed, as if they had gone on Christmas holiday and left everything shipshape in their absence. I continued down the hall and entered the kitchen. A dish had been left on the table, with the remains of dinner. It was surely Diane who had used it—who else? But why, if she'd gone on holiday this evening, hadn't she washed and put away the dish before leaving? What puzzled me even more was that the garbage hadn't been taken out. I left the kitchen and was in the hall when I heard the elevator start up on the landing. Someone had just called it back down. I stood there, stock still in the hall, unable to decide whether to retreat to the kitchen or go out the front door. I heard the elevator make its characteristic hiccup as the cabin reached the ground floor, and, immediately afterward, the winch started up again and the elevator began climbing back toward the fourth floor. Diane was in the cabin, perhaps looking at herself in the mirror. In just a few more seconds, the elevator would stop, and she would open the door and see me, I who had no business being here. For, even if this was my home—mine as much as hers, this apartment we'd rented together, the rent for which I still paid—I was perfectly aware that I had no right to be here when she wasn't. It occurred to me to try to find something to say relating to my father's death, something she couldn't object to, couldn't hold against me. I could tell her I needed to get some papers, our marriage certificate, for example, and that, passing by the house, and since I had the key, I thought I'd come up and get it. I ran to the living room to fetch our marriage certificate in the drawer where I knew it would be, and rushed back to the entryway to greet Diane. My excuse was ready, but I didn't get to use it, as Diane never showed. I heard the elevator continue up another floor or two, then stop; I heard the door open, someone come out and go home.

For more than a minute after that, I heard not a sound. Once my moment of irrational panic had passed, I came to my senses and calmly went to return the marriage certificate to the drawer where I'd found it. I crossed the room in the opposite direction, quietly. I saw the four green LEDs of the Livebox, three steady and one flickering in the dark.

The living room was bathed in a lunar light. It had been a while since I'd set foot in that living room. I noticed that there were still damp spots on the walls, a few flakes of paint hanging from the ceiling—vestiges of a leak that had poisoned our lives the previous spring, during our final months of living together. The leak, insidious rather than drastic, came from the apartment above us, no question about it, but the apartment was unoccupied, and the various contractors called to the building had been unable to locate the source. I don't remember whether Diane or I had been the first, one morning, to notice that the ceiling was dripping and had put a pot on the wood floor to deal with the most urgent crisis. At first it had just been persistent dampness, a few stagnant droplets pearling up in suspension on the ceiling; then a rosary of drips had begun falling to the floor, unstoppable, in two or three places. We had set pails and basins all along the wall, but soon the leak got worse. The ceiling had been affected in multiple places, and the section above the library was threatening to collapse. When I realized my books were in danger, I had taken matters in hand. I went to the storage area where we kept our tools, unearthing a large cylinder of bubble wrap. Armed with rolls of tape and scissors, I began cutting long strips of bubble wrap, which I taped to the corners of the bookshelves, suturing them together with more tape. I diligently fashioned a waterproof patchwork to protect my books. I had spent nearly two hours making this transparent casing, which looked like a coat by Martin Margiela, made of bits and pieces, multicolored scavenged materials and strips of adhesive tape stuck on haphazardly. When Diane came home and saw my handiwork, before she had even removed her raincoat, she said nothing, only stared at me in mute consternation. It had already been a week that we weren't talking. We came and went in the apartment without saying a word to one another, crossed paths in silence in the living room, amid the pails, basins, pots, and floorcloths. We lived parallel lives, bailing our way out; the state of the living room mirrored that of our faltering marriage. In the morning, before leaving for the Commission, I spent ten minutes emptying the pails in the kitchen sink and putting them back where the leak was heaviest. Diane did the same. We did everything each on our own, without method or coordination. Even the twins, who you would have thought would be delighted by the presence of this aquatic garden in the living room, didn't have the heart to run barefoot through the puddles and splash each other. Like us, they remained extinguished and worn down, enduring the stifling atmosphere in the apartment.

It was that crumbling apartment that we left behind early in the summer to bring the children to my parents' vacation home in Tuscany. Since the age of four, the twins had spent their holidays there; it was a family ritual, starting with Alessandro, then continuing with Henri and Hugues, my brother's children, and now it was Thomas and Tessa whom my parents welcomed every summer to Tuscany, where my father, when he was still hale and hearty, would spray them with the garden hose and inculcate them into the joys of democracy. Whereas grandfathers, in our family, had always been called "Pop-pop," my father preferred to be called "Grandfather" by his grandchildren. And just as Ravel, when he'd written *La Valse*, had added no qualifiers—there was no point, he had written *the* waltz, and to his mind there was no other—my father had deemed it needless to add further precisions. He wasn't *a* grandfather, but *the* grandfather. He had arrogated to himself the generic label and adopted its robe, customs, and prerogatives. He was the grandfather, definitive and absolute, the quintessence and pride of his homologues (not to say the star of the profession). This past year, my father's state of health had made us hesitate about sending the twins to my parents' for the holidays, but my mother had insisted that we not change a thing in our habits. The trip had been wearing for my father, and we found him visibly weakened when we arrived in Tuscany. He was sitting alone at the large cast-iron table on the terrace. I remembered him sitting in that same spot in the summer of 1999, when he was preparing for his interview to become a European commissioner, his files open before him, his journals and books, his glasses, his transistor radio, his typewriter. My father was a man of the twentieth century; he had never gotten used to a computer and instead typed his speeches on an old portable Olivetti. He started using a computer when he became a commissioner, but only by proxy, delegating its use to his chief of staff in Breydel and to my mother at home; although eventually—haltingly, cautiously, with a dark and suspicious look on his face—he took his first solitary steps toward the spanking new iMac G3 we had given him.

In 1999, my father was in the prime of life. That summer, he had before him the stimulating prospect of preparing his public audition before the European Parliament. The stakes were high, and he was absorbed and excited by the challenge. At the time, he'd annoyed me with his way of hogging attention and spreading his papers all over the table, but with distance, I can't help thinking back on it fondly when I remember his elation, which no doubt belied a slight but genuine apprehension. Despite his vast professional experience, my father felt a bit of stage fright owing to the solemnity of the exercise, which was to take place in an amphitheater that could hold four hundred people and would be broadcast live. He referred to his audition by the English term *hearing*, on the analogy of a U.S. Senate confirmation, and when speaking, somewhat pompously, of his *hearing* (which moreover he pronounced *herring*), he affected studentesque lingo, in an attempt to make a connection with his sons, and called it his "final exam." At the table, he would talk about it jokingly, as if to ward off something that he especially shouldn't say or do during his performance, like get the hiccups, which had suddenly caught him one morning. (Just imagine if I got the hiccups during my *herring*! he exclaimed with delighted horror, and he laughed in anticipation of the effect that getting hiccups would have on the amphitheater.) Throughout that summer of 1999, all he talked about was his audition, and even though I had spent only a week in Tuscany, I wasn't sorry to get out of there and leave my father to his "fish."

There was a sharp contrast between that father, at the summit of his career, happy in his professional and family life, in harmony with his sons, joking around with Alessandro, and the weakened old man that we now found when we arrived in San Donato. I was struck, leaning over to kiss him hello, to see how thin his arms had become. Even his wrists looked thinner, and the thought flashed through my mind that he must have had to tighten his watchstrap by another notch or two to keep if from slipping off. Less than two decades had passed between those two images: my father in the prime of life, about to be anointed a European commissioner; and as he was today, still sitting at the large cast-iron table, but with medications, vials, and pillboxes lined up in front of him instead of books and folders. And, pondering these two milestones in my father's life, a mere fifteen years apart, I wondered whether there wasn't some hidden truth in that image, a startling abridgment of life, the span and destiny of a person's life.

Many things had changed in those fifteen years, but on one point, at least, my father had remained true to himself—I could tell even that first evening, as the odor of citronella tickled my nostrils in the humid San Donato night—and that was the effort, foresight, and obsessiveness that went into preserving his skin from mosquito bites. When my father traveled to Tuscany, he always brought with him an arsenal of anti-mosquito products, which didn't keep him from occasionally adding a new item to his panoply, unearthed in the shadows of an old Tuscan shop, some grocery-cum-hardware store, cruising among the shelves like an eager connoisseur, taking out his reading specs to read the label of an unfamiliar and untried product. The cornerstone of his protection system was of course the good old insect repellent plug-in. He had two or three different types, and every evening, in every room of the house, he would fervently insert, as if it were a host in a communicant's mouth, the pale blue tablet into the slot of the vaporizer. For the terrace, he opted instead for a coil or spiral, earth-colored or pine green, that he balanced in a saucer, lighting one end with a match before sitting back down to let it slowly consume itself while exhaling invisible and fleeting vapors of incense into the warm Tuscan night. For outside the home, he had a bagful of mobile defenses, a whole portable arsenal of vials, sprays, and lotions, which he brought with him to the restaurant or to friends' houses, delicately coating his ankles and wrists until the atmosphere was scented with an unpleasant fragrance of citronella. I don't know where he'd picked up this obsession with combatting mosquitoes, but he had become its paragon, and the family, in his presence, never had anything to fear from Nematocera; never did the tender epidermis of the twins, their little buttocks and chubby backs, have to dread the presence of a wandering mosquito when they slept over at San Donato, under the vigilant and protean shield set up by my father.

That evening, we ate dinner on the terrace, the glow from the lamp casting a dim, tawny light. My mother had made veal with olives, and my father, who presided at the head of the table, gaunt and with taut features, drew upon his last reserves of strength to appear companionable. I watched him banter with Diane, whose female presence at his side he appreciated as much as, if not more than, her particular personality (in fact, he'd never really gotten along with Diane, who intimidated him a bit). I myself had never felt comfortable in my parents' presence. I always felt apprehensive when going to visit them, whether on Avenue Emile Duray or in Tuscany, and that feeling of fragility only increased when Diane was with me. But Diane, during this trip, and I was grateful to her for it, put aside our private disputes when with my parents. Of course, she had done only the strict minimum, but she did it well, and I couldn't ask for more. For two days, we wandered like sleepwalkers in the San Donato house, helping my mother set the table and cook the meals, while the twins limply rang the wind chimes in that overly large garden and on that terrace haunted by illness. But Diane had laid down her conditions for the stay: two days and no more, and she didn't want to spend a single night with my parents in the San Donato house. I therefore took a hotel room in Poggibonsi, a fifteen-minute drive away, which we returned to in our rental car in the evenings after dinner. The moment we left the house, the tension between us returned and immediately crested, as if Diane, having held in her acrimony for the entire evening, unleashed it on me the minute we were alone. During those two days in Tuscany, I had constantly walked in circles in my parents' garden, unable to read, unable to work, forcing myself to sit with my father for a moment at the large table. Paradoxically, the atmosphere in San Donato seemed lighter, or less unbearable, than the insufferable pall that settled in the minute I found myself alone with Diane. The two nights in the hotel in Poggibonsi, a charmless place set off from the highway, were as trying for Diane as they were for me. Her hostile presence was almost palpable in that hotel room, where we nonetheless had to coexist, without talking or touching. There was a physical awkwardness when we crossed paths, trying to avoid each other, in the 200 square feet of that hotel room. In the morning, we opened our eyes to find the other one next to us in the bed, and we got up, only half-awake, to shower by turns. We dressed next to the unmade bed, a bath towel around our haunches, encumbered by our nudity, in that anonymous room with its ruffled cotton pistachio-green curtains. We were confined to our close quarters, forced to share, for two nights running, the double bed, the bathroom, the toilets. The last day, when we went by San Donato to wish my parents goodbye, I had seen an unusual sadness in the twins' eyes. Despite their young age, there was much they had guessed: my father's illness, the state of our marriage, the silent tension hovering over San Donato. I could feel they were affected by it, and I can still see their dark, withdrawn faces in the garden when we left the property.

Diane and I had planned to spend a night in Siena before returning to Brussels, but we canceled the hotel and changed our plane tickets to fly back to Belgium that evening. Up to Siena, the ambiance in the car was electric. Diane limited herself to brief remarks about my driving. Sitting stiff and tense beside me, flinching at every intersection, she thrust her arm toward the windshield to counter a nonexistent impact and kept telling me to be careful. I don't remember how things got out of hand, but at a certain moment, exasperated, I screeched to a halt on the side of the road, in a kind of open area of packed earth surrounded by olive trees, and got out of the car. I breathed in slowly, feeling oppressed and short of breath. Diane got out as well, took a few steps, and, at the first words she said—again about my driving, specifically about having passed a cyclist recklessly and without keeping enough lateral distance (or flashing my turn signal)—no longer able to stand her complaints, exasperated by the sound of her voice, I walked away down the road. I walked along the shoulder. I could feel the warm air vibrating around me, the presence of the sun on my skin, heard the buzzing of insects in the tall grass by the roadside. It was hot, cars zipped by me, sometimes brushing so close that I could feel the wind currents. I walked for several minutes to calm down, then went back. Diane was waiting for me, sitting behind the wheel of the rental car with the door open, and the radio was turned up full, absurdly sending an Italian song to dissipate into silent nature. I opened the passenger door and took a seat next to Diane, leaving her the wheel if it meant that much to her. I leaned over and turned off the radio without asking, peremptorily, which underscored the symbolic violence between us. She started up and we continued on our way. Diane drove in silence. She had put on her glasses, which she wore only to drive, and which gave her face an unfamiliar gravitas, an unusual severity. We drove in the shadows down a narrow tree-lined road. Sometimes, when there was a clearing, you could see in the distance a row of stone pines at the crest of a hill, and perched on it a single house with a curved tile roof. I let myself be lulled by the vineyards and olive groves of the Chianti landscape. I had almost forgotten Diane's presence at my side, and I was thinking that in the fall, when my father was feeling better, I could have lunch with him at the Rosticceria Fiorentina in Brussels, an Italian restaurant on Rue Archimède that he particularly enjoyed, or maybe even the restaurant at the Berlaymont if he felt like it. I continued to watch the road in silence, and I'm not sure why, but I told Diane of my idea to have lunch with my father after the summer. I didn't expect any particular comment from her, any sort of tacit agreement or approval; but Diane turned to me and, in a scathing tone, said vehemently, "Don't you see he's dying?"

I was still in the living room on Rue de Belle-Vue, staring at the empty bookcases, their shelves devoid of books, their smooth white wood standing out in the dark. It had been more than six months since I'd emptied out our library, after having tried swathing it in bubble wrap, and I noticed it was still empty. Nothing had happened since the previous May; the books must still have been in my study, packed in boxes where I'd left them. An insurance appraiser must have come by in the interim to assess the damage, draw up estimates. Appointments must have been made, but nothing had budged since summer. Things had dragged on and the walls still hadn't been repainted. I left the living room and entered the hallway toward the darker rooms of the apartment. It felt strange to walk into the bedroom. I made out the shapes of furniture in the half-light. It was here that I'd slept with Diane for nearly ten years. In the final period of our relationship, we more or less symbolically split up the apartment. After dinner, when the twins were in bed, I would come in here to read while Diane commandeered the living room with her magazines, tablet, and TV. I had come back only once to Rue de Belle-Vue since summer, to pick up a few belongings when I moved into Place du Châtelain. I had taken the minimum, two or three suits, half a dozen shirts, and a few ties crammed into a suitcase. In the bedroom, pensive, I opened the door to the half of the closet where I had kept my clothes. A dozen or so suits hung in the shadows. The shirts were stacked on a shelf, ironed and folded. I opened the other closet door, and it was as if a fireworks display jumped out at me in the dark, a silent explosion of color: poppy, ruby, plum, lilac, an exhaustive palette of silvery blues and grays, midnight blue, cobalt blue—dozens of neckties that I'd left there, hanging in the darkness on the tie rack in a muted bouquet of colors and textures, patterns and fabrics, linen, silk, solid, polka dot, striped. Most of these ties had been chosen by Diane, who, in the early days of our marriage, had, with taste and determination, taken my physical appearance in hand and built me a new wardrobe. She had ordered custom suits for me in Brussels and Paris, we had bought shirts together in London and Venice, and, whenever she could, she would buy me a new tie; it was her guilty pleasure, and she couldn't wait to knot it sensuously around my neck. I had met Diane during what had been a period of professional fulfillment for me, having just started at the Commission. Before that, I'd been working for Futuribles in Paris, living in a studio near Rue Saint-Sabin and never giving much thought to my appearance. Though I was forty years old, I still felt like a student in work and at play. And then, in the early 2000s, I joined the European Commission and married Diane in rapid succession. After several years of indecisive wavering, I had finally found my path, and Diane's presence at my side, in the happy period of our relationship, had given me self-assurance. I felt validated next to her, elegant. In one fell swoop, as the new century began, I walked into the Berlaymont with this lovely woman on my arm.

From the start, there had been a total lack of communication between us. Moreover, the first word Diane ever said to me was, "What?" We laughed about it later, but I could have read it as an omen. It was in the hubbub of a party thrown by a Commission colleague. We had happened to find ourselves standing together at the buffet table. I knew her by sight but had never spoken to her. I pointed out the row of bottles my colleague had chosen to accompany the buffet and made a sarcastic remark about all the wines being Argentinian. It was then that I heard Diane's voice for the first time. What? she'd said, putting her hand on my arm to let me know that she hadn't heard me in the ambient cacophony. When you work for the Commission, I said louder, you've got an embarrassment of choices in terms of wine you can offer your guests: Argentinian, Chilean, Australian, Californian. She smiled. That's true, she said, he could have tried a bit harder! Don't get me wrong, I like Malbec, I added, leaning closer to talk into her ear over the music, and we started chatting about wines, vintages, regions. Diane knew her stuff. Continuing our private conversation, first standing at the buffet, then sitting, she on an elegant cane chair, me on the arm of a sofa, with a plate of hors d'oeuvres and two very handsome stem glasses that I occasionally went to refill with Malbec, we didn't leave each other's side for the rest of the evening. I was under her spell, having already noticed that she was very beautiful, and I now discovered that she was also engaging. Glasses in hand, we talked, we laughed, we tried out a few vague dance steps facing each other, a few slow, confederate pelvic movements. A little after midnight, we left the party together. Where should we go now? We had just left the apartment, and I followed her down the stairs. I proposed she come by my place, but she preferred that we go to hers. She had a small apartment in Uccle, and the magic of the evening continued in her living room. Would you like a drink? she asked once I was seated, leaning back on her large white sofa. We gently clinked glasses. She stood up, put on some music. Would you like to take a bath? she asked, standing behind me, in the same tone that she'd used to ask if I wanted a drink. I lifted my eyes toward her, interrogatively. I'm taking one, she said, and you're welcome to join. She smiled. I smiled back, and she went to run the bath. Slowly, taking her time, she walked into her room and started getting undressed, all the while continuing to talk to me from a distance. She poked her head back into the living room, in a robe, and smiled at me before returning to the bathroom. I heard her move around the room, take off her bathrobe, and step into the water. Are you coming? she said after a moment. The bathroom door had remained open. I stood up and joined her. I remained standing in the doorway, glass in hand. We looked at one another and pursued our conversation. I went out of the room. In the hallway, hesitantly, I started undressing, taking off my jacket, my tie, my shirt, which I folded over a chair. It was when it was time to remove the rest that I started feeling self-conscious. I took off my trousers and returned to the bathroom in my shorts, uncertain. I removed my shorts in a sudden motion (the art of removing your shorts in public) and joined her in the tub. Getting into the bath, I said something like, "My apologies, I left my bathing suit at home," and the flash of a smile lit her lovely eyes. What impressed me was her self-possession in the tub. Her breasts above the water, one hand resting on the edge, she looked at me as if she'd been doing this all her life. For my part, I was very ill at ease, I couldn't find my bearings. Already, when I'd sat in the tub, the level had risen considerably and a little water had spilled over onto the tile floor. I didn't move, remained frozen, and I wondered whether it was more polite for me to have a hard-on or not, to acknowledge her nudity. I had no experience in this. I opted—insofar as one can adjust one's penis as if it were the hot water tap—for a median erection, neither triumphant, which might have seemed premature, nor the total unflappability of the limp dick, which could have been taken as a lack of interest. We thus continued our conversation, facing each other in the tub, me with my appropriate semi-erection (truly well calculated; I was proud of myself). I noticed that she had, now and again, glanced down furtively to appreciate the level, which seemed to suit her just fine (we were indeed worldly folk). Until that moment, I had remained completely frozen in position, a bit awkward, at my end of the tub, not venturing out of my territory, not daring to make a movement for fear of splashing more water onto the floor. She remained at ease, turned the knob with two fingers for a moment to add some hot water, then closed the tap, with posed, elegant gestures. She delicately pressed the sponge to let a trickle of water run sensuously down her shoulder, and handed me a massage glove. Gradually I relaxed. I even dared, prudently, to unfold my limbs, which were starting to cramp in the lukewarm water. I began to feel more assured. I stretched out my foot and, delicately, eyes lowered, as if taking her hand for the first time (which, no doubt out of shyness, I still hadn't done), I slid the tip of my toe into her vagina. I made not another movement, looked her in the eye, gauging her reaction—less than a year later, we were married.

I hadn't left the bedroom of the Rue de Belle-Vue apartment, and I was still staring at my ties in the closet when my attention was drawn by a silk tie with a tiny polka-dot pattern in mauve. It was a tie my parents had given me for Christmas several years earlier. I knew it was my father who had chosen it. My father had the touching habit, when presenting a gift he had selected himself, of making a big deal of it, handing it over personally, waiting for the recipient to open it, and anxiously awaiting their reaction; he took an endearing if egotistical pleasure when we showed appreciation. When I recognized that tie in the closet among the dozens that Diane had given me, I decided to take it with me so I could wear it the next day to my father's funeral. I lifted it from the tie rack, folded it carefully, and slipped it into my jacket pocket. I was about to leave the room, but I lingered a moment by the bed. It was there, in this bed, that Diane and I had loved each other. The bed, as best I could see in the dark, was made up, the two pillows, mine and hers, standing out like whitish stains, and I wondered whether Diane, now that I was no longer there, sometimes added my pillow to hers for extra thickness, or wedged it against her chest or between her legs at night. I looked at the bed in the twilight, thinking that it was there, in the spring, that we had made love for the last time. It was an evening in May. Diane had just taken a bath—Diane always loved taking baths, she took them morning and evening (and even late at night, as when we first met). She liked taking baths in the dark, by the light of a candle that she set on the edge of the tub, listening to classical music on her tablet. That evening, after her bath, Diane had come into the bedroom, hair still wet and holding a towel, wrapped in her thick white robe. I was reading in my armchair and had smiled at her. There had been no animosity between us that evening; I shut my book and left her the room so she could have privacy. I went to brush my teeth in the bathroom, and then, seeing the tub still full, with the candle in a saucer on the edge of it, I stepped into Diane's bath and took a shower, still standing, feet and calves in the lukewarm water. Leaving the tub, I put on my robe, taking the candle with me, its flame flickering down the hall, and joined Diane in the bedroom redolent of damp and shampoo. I put the candle on the bedstand and turned off the light. We were both in our robes, she in white and I in black. The candle cast a soft light over the bedroom, and our shadows danced in slow motion on the walls. I don't know how we ended up moving toward each other, seeking contact rather than fleeing it, as we had had been doing instinctively lately when we found ourselves in the same room; how we each tentatively made a tender gesture toward the other's body, a furtive contact, the brush of a fingertip, facing each other and stopping in the middle of the room, and then understanding each other with a glance and sitting on the bed, letting ourselves fall backward together in the quilty softness of the comforter. Our robes opened, fell, slid, mine to the floor at the foot of the bed, hers on the side, still held in place by her body. What was so touching about that embrace was that we were doing our best to reach each other, do it right, renew contact through tenderness, rediscover the person that we had each kept at bay for so long. We knew how hard it was, how much stood between us, how distant we had grown these past months. We forced ourselves to become reacquainted with the other's skin, to give each other warmth, soothe one another by our embrace, even if we didn't feel any real desire—and ultimately that was what was most pathetic, most inexorably pathetic: that neither of us felt desire, that the desire between us was gone, that we settled for the age-old gestures of love, and that it was impossible, that evening, for us to set aside our mutual irritation. There was too much friction between us, which we labored to contain, to repress with our kisses and caresses, that we did our best to silence and appease, but that was ready to come surging back and explode in our faces at the slightest spark. There was nothing we could do about it, it wasn't in our control, it wasn't even our choice: we made love knowing that we had no real wish to make love, we both knew it, and yet we were so familiar with each other's bodies that we kept on with the caresses we had shared so many times before. I don't know what she was thinking at that moment, I don't even know what I was thinking, but I was acutely aware of this radical impossibility, aware that I had no desire to make love with her that evening, while we continued sucking at each other, lying head to foot in the dark. No doubt my body felt pleasure, no doubt my cock was getting off, but my soul was elsewhere, and I'm sure it was the same for her, who must have been experiencing the same aporia as I sucked on her pussy in the twilight. We saw only each other's sex organs in the candlelight; no doubt it was more neutral and impersonal, simpler than if we had been joined face-to-face, than if, in our kisses, we'd had to face the other's distraught mouth and implacable stare. And just then she made a movement, which I took as a sign of annoyance or irritation: she lifted her pelvis impatiently to try to remove a flap of her bathrobe that had remained stuck under her buttock, that must have been bothering her and that she wanted to be rid of, brusquely, unceremoniously. It wasn't me she was irritated with but that flap of robe, but by moving to rid herself of it, twisting under me in ill humor, she had at the same time pushed me away to yank on it, pull it out from under her buttock. And though she hadn't said a word, that movement in itself had betrayed her, had starkly revealed how she felt about me; her movement had borne witness to her fundamental irritation at being with me at that moment in our conjugal bed. And I seized upon that clear, implicit confession to disengage, put an end to our pointless embrace. I immediately stopped what I was doing, rolled to the side of the bed and stretched out on my back, yanking on the sheets in my own annoyance to cover the nakedness that I no longer felt like sharing with her. What I then said to her I didn't really mean; I said it to rid myself of her, to keep her at a distance, to wound her. What I then said to her was that she didn't know how to do it. I don't think I said anything else, only that she didn't know how to do it, but it was more than enough, more than she could bear to hear; no one can stand to hear that from a lover, even if "knowing how to do it" isn't really the issue, and has never been the point of love and sexual relations when two people love each other. Why, because *you* do? she retorted. No, not me, I don't know how to do it either, neither of us knows how to do it, I said, trying to backtrack. I immediately felt in the wrong, guilty, at fault. Slowly, Diane unfolded her nude body on the mattress, planted her feet on the floor, sitting on the edge of the bed with her back to me. She didn't say a word, and I understood her dejection, her hurt. I wanted to do something, not to pardon myself, but to show compassion for what we had become, and I leaned over toward her, gently touched her arm. She shook me off violently. She sat on the edge of the bed, not moving. Then she turned around to look at me. She stared at me for a long time, her expression impenetrable and her eyes cold, and she seemed deep in thought. Her face, in the candlelight, was very beautiful, very determined. I had never seen her so ardent. It was terrible to behold. And then, in a flat voice, not even argumentative, she delivered the fruits of her reflection. I don't love you, she said.

◆

We heard a knock at the door of my father's study. Before we had time to react, the door opened and the funeral director entered, walked softly toward us, and said in an obsequious voice, "We shall now proceed with the closing of the casket." I felt a squeeze in my heart, and abruptly I understood what that meant. Perhaps the family would like to pay its respects one final time? We nodded in silence. Pierre left the study to let the children know, and I don't know how word spread in the house, but we began to hear voices from the distance, whispers, the sound of muffled steps in the hall, and, almost immediately, Pierre's sons came into the room, heads lowered, feeling awkward, soon followed by Alessandro and the twins: Thomas in a proper young man's blazer and Tessa in a blue dress with white trim. Suddenly, after the long, meditative silence in that room since early morning, there was movement in my father's study. The funeral director had left us to ourselves. Thomas and Tessa, having asked my permission, each lit a candle and came back toward us, eyes glued to the flame, concentrating, to go stand guard on either side of my father's casket. My father lay to rest before us in the open casket, in suit and tie, hands crossed over his stomach. I looked at his motionless face over which danced the reflections of the candle flames, and I knew that it was the last time I would see him, that this would be my last image of him. After that, I left the study and went back to the living room. I stood at the window, my gaze vacant, watching the rain falling on the street. The hearse was parked in front of the house, visible through the glass. Alessandro came to stand next to me at the bay window, and I tried to smile, made an affectionate gesture toward him, the gesture a father makes toward his son—and I realized, with a slight feeling of vertigo, that in father–son relationships, I was now only a father.

The funeral director reappeared to say that the procession could now get underway. There was more movement in the living room; everyone stood up from their seats and started putting on their coats. I greeted Sylvie, my brother's wife, who had just arrived. I watched the casket being ceremoniously taken from the study, carried on the shoulders of four silhouettes in dark suits. They went through the French doors of the dining room and turned toward the vestibule; we stood aside to allow them passage. The funeral director, walking ahead, opened the front door, and we followed the casket into the street, buttoning up our coats against the chill air of December. Everyone split up into various cars to head to the church. There were barely five hundred yards between my parents' house and La Cambre Abbey, so I decided to go on foot. It was drizzling, and there was frost on the roofs of the cars. After a moment, I saw the funeral procession pass by me, slowly making its way down Avenue Emile Duray, hearse in the lead, followed by my brother's car with my mother inside. When I entered the main courtyard, the hearse was slowly circling the paved path that skirted the white structure of the abbey palace. The car stopped at the door of the church, where some fifty people were already waiting. Lost in thought, I crossed the courtyard toward the church. People were standing by the doorway in small clusters, beneath umbrellas. I recognized a number of faces watching me approach, with sober, discreet, blank expressions. I felt somewhat empty, and at the same time the center of attention. I greeted a few people, made my way through the crowd, through hugs and embraces, shaking hands, exchanging a few words. Many of my parents' friends were there, some having made the trip from Paris.

When I pushed open the door of Notre-Dame de la Cambre, the first person I saw in the shadow of the entryway was Elisabetta, my first wife. Alessandro had said that his mother would be present for the service, and it gave me great pleasure to find her there. Elisabetta had flown in from Rome that morning. She hadn't had time to leave her bags at the hotel. She had taken a taxi from the airport, but the driver had made a mistake, dropped her at the church of Sainte-Croix instead, and she'd had to walk for a quarter of an hour in the rain. She had taken off her wet raincoat and folded it over a prie-dieu to let it drip. When I entered the church, she was squatting on the floor and rummaging through a large travel bag, pulling out clothes and placing her toiletry kit on the stone tiles. She had no doubt prepared an outfit for the funeral, but, having no time to change, she contented herself with exhuming from the depths of her bag an elegant tan-and-black silk scarf that she knotted around her neck for the ceremony. When she saw me, she stood up and came over, her face grief-stricken, and we hugged. She raised her face to look at me and said in a murmur, "I loved him very much, you know. I always loved your father." Elisabetta cried on my shoulder, I felt the warm contact of her body against mine, and I was flustered by that embrace that had something soft and sensual about it. Taking my arm, she gathered up her scattered belongings and walked ahead of me into the nave, carrying her overnight bag. She spotted my mother from a distance, standing in the front pew accepting condolences from one of my father's former colleagues, and gave her a discreet wave. My mother's eyes, which seemed vacant in an expressionless face, lit up for a moment when she recognized Elisabetta. I could tell she was happy to see her, that she was grateful to her for coming all the way from Rome. Elisabetta went toward my mother, and I saw them embrace wordlessly in the front pew. They were sobbing in each other's arms, but already, Elisabetta, wiping away her tears, told my mother about her misadventures with the taxi, and, punctuating her story with who knows what supplemental mishaps, she began to laugh, and we could hear Elisabetta's hearty, light, joyful laugh echo in the solemn silence of the church. My mother, smiling and weeping at the same time, looked at Elisabetta, slightly taken aback, slightly disconcerted (as for Alessandro, looking smart in his black jacket and white shirt, he looked at his mother with a mix of pride and affection). The funeral director then invited us to take our seats for the start of the ceremony, but Elisabetta didn't budge, heedless of his directives. She continued to chat with my mother in the front pew, her back to the altar, travel bag by her feet. Elisabetta had never really paid attention to rules or followed instructions. She gaily freed herself from proprieties, but she did it so naturally and so casually that each time she seemed to be creating a new convention for her own personal use, as if, instead of respecting rules, she completely transcended them.

Elisabetta had always gotten along well with my parents, with my father in particular, even though they had very different personalities. My father, a stickler for ethics, had taught Pierre and me, from the time we were little, about the founding principles of democracy, the separation of powers, plurality of opinions, majority rule, the fairness principle. To my mind, those principles were beyond dispute or discussion, like certain universal laws of physics. The fairness principle, for instance, as related to daily life, might concern how to share something, a slice of cake or cut of meat. The principle, the golden rule that my father had always taught us, could be elegantly summarized in the axiom: "One person cuts, the other person chooses." To me, that seemed absolutely sensible, easy to understand, and it limited any temptation toward abuse, obliging the person sharing to try for the greatest equity, at the risk of ultimately shortchanging himself. But Elisabetta didn't see things that way. When we had only one piece of chocolate cake in the house to share for dessert, Elisabetta, with great naturalness, not to say gluttony, split the cake into two manifestly unequal portions and helped herself to the larger one, biting into it with clear gusto. To my outraged protests, as I sputtered in indignation at this blatant breach of democracy, she laughed heartily and went, "Oh, you're not going to make a whole song and dance over an extra bite of cake, are you?" And if I insisted, trying to explain that it was obviously not just about the small extra bit of cake she'd purloined but about the principle—the universal principle of democracy that had to be defended wherever it was under threat, anywhere in the world—she gave me a coquettish wink that might have meant, "I'll make it up to you," and even, on good days, "I'll make it up to you in the sack." That has nothing to do with it, I protested, and besides, you're trying to corrupt me! She was mixing up sex and equity! Elisabetta's eyes, still merry, seemed to add, "You won't lose anything by waiting." I was appalled. She didn't even realize that it was democracy itself she was murdering.

Another of my father's principles that Elisabetta casually brushed aside was salt. My father had always recommended to my brother and me, then to his grandchildren (I know: to my surprise, I had seen Tessa, from the vast experience of her nine years, scrupulously apply my father's principle one time when she was making crepes), never to salt directly from the box into the dish being cooked, but always—always—to pass by the hand, to first pour the salt into your hand, the better to dose it correctly and avoid the catastrophe of too much salt dissolving into the food. It was a sensible principle; I had explained it to Elisabetta over and over. But how many times, in our little Paris kitchen, had I caught her, in front of a delicate fish that she was cooking in the pan, pouring on salt from the box—what am I saying, happily turning the box upside down over the fish and shaking it, with all her passionate, Latinate ardor, ready to send me packing if I uttered so much as a word?

I watched Elisabetta in the church and, seeing her as she had always been—open, radiant, sunny—I recalled our first meeting nearly thirty years earlier. That summer, Elisabetta had come to restore a chapel near my parents' house in Tuscany. We had had dinner one evening with a group of friends. Elisabetta told us that she'd just completed her art history studies and that this was her first professional experience. Curious to know more about her work, I asked if I could visit her, and she told me which bus I needed to take. It was a Romanesque chapel, partially in ruins, in the Pisan style, standing alone at the side of a road. When I ventured inside on my first visit, passing abruptly from the blinding sun of the Tuscan countryside to the cool darkness of the chapel, I found Elisabetta perched on a scaffold about five feet from the ground. She was wearing a white coat smeared with paint and had a magnifying visor pushed back up her forehead. She came down from the scaffold to greet me, and I noticed that she was wearing around her neck a gold chain with a minuscule baptism medallion. I came to see her again the next day, and several times more the following week. Elisabetta got used to my presence. I sat on the stone floor in a corner of the chapel, watching her without a word. We didn't speak much. There were long silent pauses during which she worked on her fresco, kneeling on the scaffolding, delicately scraping at the layer of paint with the tip of a scalpel, sometimes pulling the magnifying visor down over her eyes to study a detail. I was happy just watching her, doing nothing other than being smitten, my soul filled with her beautiful and calming presence. I fell for Elisabetta at first sight, something in her laugh, the glint in her eyes, a way of looking at me with a smile that made me feel blessed by heaven. But I didn't know how to tell her. Elisabetta, leaning over her fresco, was happy to talk to me about her work, and she explained that you always had to approach the pictorial layer very cautiously, gently, delicately. Just like with love, she said, and she turned to me with a laugh. Sometimes she came down from the scaffold to take a few steps back and get perspective on what she had just done. She stopped a moment at the trestle table, a simple plank that she had set up in a corner of the chapel, which supported a hodgepodge of basins, spatulas, scalpels, and brushes. Then she climbed up the scaffold, palette in hand, and went back to work, retouching the fresco with great precision, adding a tiny dab with the tip of her brush. As much as Elisabetta, in daily life, could be capricious, in work she was meticulous. One day when she came down from her scaffold, I stood up to join her. We were side by side in the middle of the chapel, our bodies nearly touching, and Elisabetta took my arm to drag me over to the trestle table. I was unnerved by that first physical contact, which left me thrilled but unsure how to prolong it. I wanted to take her hand, but I didn't dare, and when she went back up her scaffold, I sat down in my corner. Everything that day went as usual, and I left to catch my bus. We came so close to nothing ever happening between us. And yet, it was on that day that we exchanged our first kiss. Later, thinking back on that afternoon, I always imagined Alessandro watching the scene from the balcony, observing us from Limbo, like one of Raphael's winged cherubim resting his elbows on a cloud, and wondering how the scene was going to play out, whether he would eventually be born or not. No doubt he must have thought that things were off to a poor start when I left the chapel and went to catch the bus. Moreover, I myself later wondered what might have happened if I hadn't missed it. It is often the tiny moments that are so decisive in our lives, details that turn on nothing (a choice, an impulse, a chance occurrence, a delay), the importance of which we rarely recognize at the time, but that can change the course of our destiny. Having missed the bus, I went back to the chapel. When I passed through the door, Elisabetta was waiting atop her scaffold. You're back, she said with a smile, as if she had never doubted it, and she held out her hand. I joined her on the scaffold, carefully climbing up the tubular structure, and went toward her on the walkway. There was a seriousness in her eyes. I gently took her hand, and we shared our first kiss there on the scaffold, five feet above the ground, with no other witness than pockmarked St. Francis and his birds, their colors pale and faded, on the fresco she was restoring.

My father's casket made its entrance into La Cambre Abbey. The four funeral parlor employees carrying it on their shoulders advanced slowly into the nave. I stood silently in the front pew, between my mother and Alessandro, with the twins, motionless and with heads bowed, on Alessandro's other side. Elisabetta had taken a place behind us in the second pew, and I could feel her protective presence at my back. The funeral parlor staff set the casket down in front of the altar. I knew that my father was inside, but the thought was unbearable, and I preferred to banish it from my mind in order, now and subsequently, to preserve the memory of my father alive, immaterial, unaltered. I looked at the casket placed on the catafalque, I couldn't take my eyes off it, I stared at it with painful intensity. For the living, coffins are like mirrors. My father was the one who had died, but it was my own life I was seeing in front of me as I stared vacantly. Now and then, I felt Elisabetta's hand on my shoulder, giving my collarbone a squeeze to punctuate a particularly moving moment in the service, and the presence of that warm hand on my shoulder, that affectionate contact, brought me huge comfort. My eyes still fixed on my father's casket, I was thinking that it was Elisabetta who was here with me at my father's funeral, and not Diane. My love life would surely have been much less complicated and disjointed if Elisabetta and I had not separated the first time we hit a hurdle. Maybe I should have tried harder to save our love and create a sustained relationship with her, a lifelong love affair, accepting the risks, the ups and downs, the storms and arguments (and in that regard, I could count on Elisabetta). I could or should have had that aspiration for us, rather than, at the first snag, the first infidelity, taking separation as the easy way out, giving up without a fight.

My father was dead. I said it to myself just like that: "My father is dead," and I reflected that at least the anxiety that had haunted him all his life was now being laid to rest with him. I knew that anxiety, knew it all too well, that demanding anxiety, that burning, fundamental anxiety, that anxiety for perfection that he had passed down to me and that would finally expire only with my own death. My father had always been an anxious man, often irrationally so, but he was not pessimistic. I saw a vast difference between the two: for, if pessimism is an attitude toward life, anxiety is in league with death. In both his private dealings and his public affairs, my father always looked to the positive side of things. Even in the most apparently compromised situations, his incomparable intellectual machinery cranked up to find reasons for hope. In the final months of his life, disasters had accumulated before his eyes. Terrorism had struck in the heart of Europe, in cities he loved. The day of the attacks in Brussels, he must have heard through the windowpanes of the living room on Avenue Emile Duray the sinister whine of ambulances speeding toward Maelbeek metro station. Then there had been, blow upon blow, deathblow upon deathblow, Brexit and Trump's election. My father, in his last months of life, had seen a page turn before his eyes, in which excess, slander, and mendacity had taken over the public forum, in which respect for the facts no longer had the inviolate character it had always enjoyed in the past. He had been present for the birth of a new era, in which emotion—or its caricature, for true emotions do not shout—had overridden reason. My father, already very weak, sick, dumbfounded, had remained groggy; but I'm convinced that, confronted with the shipwreck he was witnessing, he had still nurtured a secret hope, refusing to see the European ideal that he had defended all his life collapse like a house of cards.

Sometimes the death of an individual corresponds to the end of an era. Stefan Zweig died during one of history's worst moments, when the skies over Europe were blackened and the horizon blocked as far as the eye could see. Witness to the most savage triumph of brutality the world has ever known, Zweig experienced the violent intrusion of the outside world into his private universe as few intellectuals had before him. He saw his world, his familiar world, a world of reason, art, refinement, and culture, disappear literally before his eyes, while the humanism on which all his values were founded was swept aside by Nazism. Even if my father was confronted with less tragic events in the last years of his life, I saw a parallel between his death and Zweig's. The dates of their respective deaths coincided with the ebb of a wave of history, when the dawn so fervently hoped for after the long night Zweig wrote about in his final letter still hadn't risen. In a sense, we could say that Zweig and my father died at the right time, insofar as they stopped seeing the catastrophe surrounding them and didn't have to experience the disasters that ensued. But my practice of looking toward what's to come, my professional familiarity with the future, tells me that currents, once they have dipped so low, can only rise again. History, like the sea, is an eternal new beginning, an infinite recurrence of overlapping waves. Moreover, a mere six months after Zweig's death, the first rays of the expected dawn began appearing on the horizon. The Allied counteroffensive in North Africa and the victory in Stalingrad would be harbingers of the reversal starting to occur in the Second World War. I remember that, shortly before my father's death, on a day when I'd come to visit and was chatting with him in his study (it was in late November, no doubt the last time I had a conversation with him about current events), he stood up and crossed over to his desk to find a press clipping. Still standing, he read it to me aloud: "The EU is going to break up." He smiled. You know who said that? he said with an amused glimmer in his eye. Trump. He wryly put the clipping back on his desk and waved his arm as if to say, "Bah, who cares what that lowbrow says about anything." Heed this instead, he said, and he picked up another sheet of paper, a page torn out of a notebook on which I was moved to see that he had copied down a quotation. It was by Victor Hugo, and on a whole other level: "Since America, alas, is tending toward darkness in its lugubrious maintenance of servitude, let Europe once again shine a light!"

My father was buried. It was over.

I was sitting in an armchair, not moving, in the living room on Avenue Emile Duray. A lit lamp stood on the pedestal table next to me. I had no idea what the hour might be, having lost all sense of time. It was dark outside, and the last people still in the house were saying goodbye to my mother. I went to put on my coat as well and kissed my mother goodbye, telling her that I was going to spend the evening with Elisabetta, who was only in Brussels for two days. I was taking her and Alessandro to dinner. A taxi came to pick us up, and I helped Elisabetta put her travel bag in the trunk, an elegant blue leather bag that had suddenly grown rather heavy, following who knows what private arrangement between her and Alessandro. I gathered that she had taken the six volumes of a history of art in Italian that she had lent him while he was studying at La Cambre, and apparently she had found nothing more important that evening than to pack them up so she could bring them back to Rome. The taxi dropped us off at Place du Sablon. Walking down the street toward the restaurant, I pulled off my tie, folded it carefully, and put it in my pocket. You're much handsomer without a tie, Elisabetta said, taking my arm. I don't like you in ties, she added, you look like a—and she tried to find the word. Like a Eurocrat, Alessandro said with a smile, giving his mother a wink to affectionately make fun of me. *Ma si, è vero!* Elisabetta said with a laugh. Let's not have any populism, I said with an impish smile. Even though the circumstances that evening were painful for the three of us, we were happy to be together again; it had been a long time since we'd been able to share a dinner out. After having studied art in Rome, Alessandro had gotten a master's in typography in Brussels. At present he lived on his typographical productions, creating letterforms for his own use and supplementing font families for a Swiss foundry, designing weights from ultra bold to extra light. He worked with a font generator software to design typographic characters in 3D, the use of which, he said, would grow exponentially in the coming years.

After dinner, Alessandro left his mother and me at Place du Sablon and went off to meet some friends in a café near the Stock Exchange. I saw Elisabetta back to her hotel. She was tired, having gotten up in Rome at six that morning to catch her plane. She'd had some wine in the restaurant, and I sensed that she was feeling slightly melancholy; in the taxi, she rested her head on my shoulder. At the hotel, I paid the driver and walked her to the reception desk, carrying the weekend bag that contained the six volumes of art history. Elisabetta checked in and got her key. I was about to leave, when she picked up her bag, then immediately set it back down on the floor. Can you help me get this to my room? she said with a disarming smile, the kind you couldn't refuse. We took the elevator to the fourth floor. Elisabetta went in first, with me following; I put the bag on the bed while she went to close the door. Normally, I don't feel ill at ease in Elisabetta's company and have always enjoyed her buoyant presence. But sometimes I had trouble interpreting her gestures, which were never clearly defined, which always seemed to exist in a zone of diffuse, ambiguous shadow. She fixed her gaze on me, and I didn't know what she was thinking. She seemed tired, but at the same time I felt that she didn't want me to leave. We were standing facing one another in her hotel room. You know, about your father, she said in a murmur, and she didn't finish her sentence. Elisabetta often didn't finish her sentences, she left the situation in suspense, creating a discomfort or an expectation for those who didn't know her. I know how you must be feeling, she said in a low voice, moving closer. She put her arms around me silently, and I recalled her embrace that morning in the church, the agitation I'd felt when she'd pressed her body against mine, her female body, soft, enveloping, and so reassuring. I was flustered, and I pressed myself against her, seeking comfort against her body; I nestled tightly into her arms, letting my emotions run free. She was moved as well, she lifted her face toward mine, seeking out my lips, and it was as if everything were occurring in a reality that was slower, almost petrified. I kissed Elisabetta and felt a great mental confusion, feelings of grief and love blending together. Kissing Elisabetta, I was filled with a completely unknown sensation, as if this were our very first kiss, or as if I was kissing a stranger in a hotel room, but at the same time it was as if my entire life were resurfacing from deep down. As if the entire history of our love were coming back to life through our lips. We fell onto the bed and continued to fondle each other. I had closed my eyes, and yet I still felt like I was about to get up and leave. I hadn't taken off my coat, I never intended to stay—for the entire duration of our embrace, I was on the verge of leaving—but I was overcome by dizziness. I had opened Elisabetta's raincoat, and there was something ineluctable in the sequence of our movements. We pressed against each other, knocking the bothersome travel bag off the bed. I didn't know what I was doing, I touched her body, she ran her hands over my neck and shoulders, I didn't know what was going on, nor do I know how it stopped—but stop it did, we stopped kissing and touching, looked at each other without moving, lying motionless on the bedspread, and it felt as if we were both at once terribly embarrassed and terribly pacified. What we had just experienced in that hotel room was inexpressible. Any attempt at explanation would have been reductive, would have denatured the unique experience we had just lived through. In fact, we had done nothing, but for me that nothing had an indescribable resonance, and the fleeting union of our bodies that night in that hotel room, even if we had soon broken it off, even if nothing had really happened, had been one of the most deeply moving embraces of my entire life. Thank you for coming to Brussels, I said to her. I'll always be here, she said. I'll always be here for you.

Leaving the hotel, I returned home on foot. It was no more than fifteen minutes away. Still dazed by what I had just experienced with Elisabetta, I walked through the deserted streets of Brussels. I was skirting the Ixelles Ponds and was about to head up toward Avenue Louise to get to

Place du Châtelain when, as I entered Rue de Belle-Vue, I noticed that there was still a light on in Diane's apartment. I slowed down and gazed at the building. But, fearing I'd be seen, as I was standing in the open, I crossed the esplanade to station myself on the other side of the street. I stopped near the fence of another building from where I couldn't be observed. I was watching the window on the fourth floor when I saw a shape moving in the living room, and I immediately knew it was Diane. But what was Diane doing at home? Hadn't she told me she was catching a plane the previous evening? Hadn't she shown me her ticket when I'd come to pick up the twins? Was she already back? She couldn't be back so soon if she'd flown out only yesterday evening. Which meant that she had never left. But then, why insist on showing me her plane ticket? I wanted to get to the bottom of this. I took out my phone and punched in Diane's number, keeping my eyes glued to the fourth-floor window. I waited, phone at my ear. Ring followed upon ring in the emptiness, and Diane didn't answer. I was certain she was hearing the phone, which must have been ringing in the living room or vibrating in her handbag, as I could see through the window that she was shaken. She had picked up her phone and seen my number on the screen; as she didn't answer, the phone must have felt like fire in her hand. I could see her shadow squirming nervously in the window frame, not sure what to do, and I could sense the intensity of her emotion and annoyance at my calling her now, at past ten o'clock at night. But still Diane didn't answer. She went to the window, and I saw her silhouette peering into the darkness. I put away my phone and, without a moment's hesitation, crossed the street toward the building. I was no longer hiding, didn't care if she recognized me walking resolutely toward her, for it was indeed to her place that I was now heading and, whether she liked it or not, we were going to talk. I needed an explanation. I knew perfectly well that when I buzzed the intercom, she might not answer, might not open the door, might simply wait from behind the curtain for me to leave—but no matter, I was going upstairs, and we were going to talk this out. She couldn't stop me: I had a key.

I crossed through the small garden and went into the dark entranceway. I rang Diane's buzzer on the intercom. I waited. Would she answer? Would I have to force my way in? I heard the crackling of the intercom, then Diane's voice saying, "Yes?" And it was the same "yes," exactly the same "yes," as when I'd called several weeks earlier, before my departure for Asia, to ask her to watch the children; that arrogant "yes" that made you feel like you were intruding before you'd even gotten a word out. It's me, I said. She asked what I wanted. I have to talk to you, I said. She didn't answer immediately. She clearly didn't want to talk to me that evening, but she couldn't find an excuse for refusing to let me in. She finally said it was late and could I come back tomorrow. No, now, I said. I said it firmly, and again I sensed her hesitate. She was weakening; I felt I had to press my advantage right away, so I trotted out my story of needing our marriage certificate for paperwork relating to my father's death. I knew that by mentioning my father's passing, it would be harder for her to refuse me entrance, and I added that I needed it for the next morning. There was another pause. She said nothing and, after a moment, I heard the click of the door being unlocked. I went through and called the elevator. At the fourth floor, I didn't turn on the hallway light. I rang the doorbell and waited in the dark. Diane opened. She had gotten the marriage certificate out for me. She handed it to me without preamble, no doubt hoping I'd leave immediately. She didn't ask me in, and her face was frozen. I took a half step forward so as not to remain in the landing, forcing her to step back, but I couldn't take a second step without knocking into her, as she was blocking the entrance. I glanced over her shoulder; the light in the living room had remained on. You know that today was my father's funeral? I said. She looked at me, motionless, arms folded. Yes, she said after a moment. Do you want to know how it went? I asked, knowing full well that she had no desire whatsoever to know how my father's funeral had gone, that her only desire was to be left alone, that the only thing she wanted was for me to go away. Still, she couldn't very well say to my face, "No, I don't care how your father's funeral went." So she said nothing, and I started to tell her about it. She listened, her face hard, arms folded over her chest. She didn't nod or give any sign of encouragement for me to go on. She listened grudgingly, a captive audience, unable to walk away and leave her home; she was forced to listen. Stop, she suddenly cried out, stop! She had held back until then, but had finally blurted it out: enough, she didn't want to hear any more. Fine. Since she didn't want to hear about the funeral, we'd get down to my real reason for coming. So, you didn't leave yesterday evening after all, I said, and I immediately saw her blanch. She was disconcerted, flustered, didn't know what to say, hadn't expected to need an excuse. She was unable to explain why she hadn't left the night before, and why, since she hadn't left, she hadn't come to my father's funeral. I'm leaving tomorrow, she said. Ah, as you always intended, I said, it's what you'd always intended, isn't it? Again I saw she was flustered. She was losing her composure. She kept silent awhile longer, then nodded. In reality, I understood only later what Diane was up to. When I'd called her on my return from Japan to tell her my father had died, Diane knew that she had no wish to attend the funeral, that she didn't want to see me, or my mother, or the family. Her winter holidays had been arranged well before that, so, since she didn't want to be at my father's funeral, she had tried to leave a few days earlier. But her ticket could not be changed, so she had bought another one, and it was that ticket she'd shown me the day before. Perhaps, at that moment, she'd even meant to take that earlier flight, but for some reason she hadn't. And what I understood later was that this new ticket was not a ruse; that plane ticket that she had indeed bought and had brandished in front of me as proof that she wouldn't be in Brussels on the day of my father's funeral had been the price she paid for not attending the funeral. With that plane ticket, she had been able to produce tangible proof that it was materially impossible for her to attend the funeral. Once the ticket had played its part, it didn't matter which flight she took, that wasn't the point: the ticket had served as her alibi, her excuse, to justify her absence at my father's funeral.

IN LIFE THERE ARE DECISIVE MOMENTS, certain days or hours that one can never forget. Stefan Zweig, in his book *Decisive Moments in History* (*Sternstunden der Menschheit*), speaks of alignments of the stars, when moments of great dramatic concentration, occurring at precise instants, carry destiny forward, condense a crucial turning point into "a single day, a single hour, and often a single minute." The French translation of Zweig's book is called *Les Très Riches Heures de l'humanité*—The Very Rich Hours of Humanity—which to my mind doesn't fully capture the idea of *kairos* that accompanies the German word *Sternstunden* (literally, "stellar moments"). These crucial moments are often public dates related to grand political or historical events, dates for which everyone knows where they were and what they were doing: July 21, 1969, when a human first walked on the moon, or the World Trade Center attacks on September 11, 2001. But such moments might involve a life-changing personal experience, most often related to sex or death. These indelible dates in our lives, dates that remain forever etched in our memories, are amplified still further if they occur alongside a huge historical event, if there is a coincidence between the life of the world and our own life. So it was with me on April 18, 2010.

After lying dormant for nearly two hundred years, the Icelandic volcano Eyjafjöll began erupting in the early hours of Wednesday, April 14, 2010. The eruption sent up an enormous cloud of steam and volcanic ash that rose to 11 kilometers above the crater. The giant plume, visible from space by the satellite Meteosat-9, first appeared black because it contained ice particles that masked the dust, then took on a reddish cast that revealed the presence of volcanic ash. This volcanic ash constituted a severe danger for air traffic because of reduced visibility, and even more so because it is composed of very hard, very corrosive particles of pulverized rock, which when sucked in by the turbines could impair the reactors, or even cause the engines to stall. These minuscule particles are also liable to interfere with the instruments associated with the pitot-static system and damage the plane's surface, including the wings and windscreen. No aircraft has ever been lost due to volcanic ash, but several serious incidents have occurred over the years. In 1982, a British Airways Boeing 747 had to make an emergency landing in Jakarta after its four reactors failed, and several other serious events occurred in Alaska in 1989. Since the planes' weather radar is unable to read concentrations of volcanic ash, the European authorities decided to shut down all flight paths.

At the time, I was working for DG MOVE, the European Commission's department of mobility and transport, and I followed the crisis daily. Since the previous Thursday, I had been working fifteen-hour shifts, returning home from the office exhausted, and my few hours of sleep were shallow and troubled. I woke up at six, and even though I checked my email every night before going to bed, other messages had come in by morning. For the past forty-eight hours, Eurocontrol had been monitoring the situation continuously, while for us at DG MOVE, the crisis really kicked in on April 14, with the closing of British air space. The following day, the ash cloud had reached the Continent, and the French, Belgian, Swedish, and Norwegian authorities followed suit. In any case, with the London and Frankfurt airports closed, very few planes could reach Europe. Thousands of flights were canceled, leaving millions of travelers stranded throughout the world. I had never known such a huge crisis in my time at the Commission. I had joined in 2004, starting in the Directorate-General for Mobility and Transport, which at the time was called Transportation and Energy. Since 2009, when the new Commission took office, I'd been liaison to the office of Siim Kallas, the Commission vice president who also dealt with transport. My primary role was interinstitutional relations. At the time the Eyjafjöll crisis broke out, we in the Commission had been working on a vast information campaign regarding passengers' rights. Safeguarding the rights of travelers was the new central axis of our political agenda, to show that Europe had a concrete, beneficial impact on the lives of its citizens (in case this might have been unclear to anyone), and the Commission had set up strict regulations governing redress for delayed or canceled flights. But suddenly we had a hundred thousand canceled flights and millions of stranded passengers on our hands. We managed at the eleventh hour to cancel our scheduled communication blitz, "Europe at Your Service": it would have looked rather silly to run full-page ads on this theme at that moment. But what were we to do about the regulation, which was very pro-passenger? Could we enforce it, at the risk of tanking the entire airline industry, or should we suspend it because of extenuating circumstances? This was clearly a case of force majeure. But force majeure, as defined legally, while it dispenses airlines from having to offer passengers a refund, nonetheless obliges them to provide lodgings, water, and meals, and to find a way of getting them to their final destination, which in itself would have been ruinous. As such, there was a lively internal debate, and an urgent need to come to a decision. Deeming that Europe would lose all credibility if it didn't maintain its protection of passengers, Siim Kallas chose to stand firm in the storm and to enforce the regulation come hell or high water. The matter was decided on Thursday evening, and a colleague and I remained in the office until one in the morning to draft the communiqué explaining the commissioner's position. We then circulated our draft to the other commissioners' offices, as all Commission resolutions are made collaboratively. The next day, at a meeting at the Berlaymont, I summarized our approach, and, in the absence of objections, we made the release public, explaining the Commission's official position vis-à-vis enforcement of the 2004 regulation on passengers' rights.

On Sunday, April 18, I left our apartment on Rue de Belle-Vue a little before nine o'clock. Diane and the twins were still asleep. I had taken my laptop with me, as, in addition to the many emergency meetings I had to attend, I was in charge of drafting the mandate. The mandate, which defined the commissioner's position (and that of the Commission in general, once ratified), is a written document called a GRI report (GRI is an acronym for Interinstitutional Relations Group). The GRI report is a strictly internal document, always structured in three sections: nature of the problem, development, proposed course of action. The document is constantly being updated. From Thursday afternoon to Saturday evening, it had been discussed and revised dozens of times, via email exchanges among the Commission's various departments. I was responsible for tracking the GRI report; I modified and amended it in real time, as the crisis developed and the positions of the member states evolved to follow it.

Arriving at my office on Rue Demot that day, I passed through the security check and took the elevator to the ninth floor. There was a lazy atmosphere of Sunday morning in the hallways; many doors were shut. I walked past the row of empty offices. The meeting was held in an impersonal conference room, with a large oval table, a few plants, and a droopy European flag hanging limply next to a flipchart. Our CEO, Manfred Hübner, was there, along with Miguel Cordoba, the director of air transports, and three in-house experts, one in charge of environmental matters, one dealing with the Single European Sky, and the third, in charge of passengers' rights, joining via Skype. But the Skype connection soon malfunctioned, and after the third expert had exchanged greetings with a few acquaintances, the connection broke up, and soon we no longer saw or heard him. He vanished with the characteristic Skype siphoning tone (a gurgle and then nothing: the expert on passengers' rights had vanished as if sucked down the software's digital drain). Moreover, he wasn't the only one absent that day. Many Commission colleagues, who had been traveling on business at the start of the crisis, couldn't get back to Brussels. Just within DG MOVE itself, despite being the most centrally concerned, several chairs remained empty. Some came late to the constant stream of emergency meetings: we saw them rush in, suitcase in hand, from Budapest or Lisbon, straight from the overnight bus that had dropped them off at dawn, unshaven, clutching hot coffee in a plastic cup. Others, who were stuck in the United States or Asia, never managed to get back to Brussels in time at all, like our unit chief in charge of air safety, who remained stranded in Philadelphia where he'd been attending a conference. Everyone had at least one friend, acquaintance, or relative who was directly affected by the flight cancellations. It was the first time we'd worked on a case that had such personal resonance. Nor was I spared, as Elisabetta and Alessandro were in the States. They had gone to check out a university where Alessandro was to spend a semester and had been stuck in Los Angeles for the past two days.

Manfred Hübner, our CEO, opened the meeting by reminding us that we were living through the worst air transit paralysis ever to hit Europe. As things stood, according to the latest reports, twenty-three countries had closed their airspace. Pressure on the Commission by the airlines to reopen the airways by Monday morning was becoming more intense with each passing hour. The airlines were suffering catastrophic losses, in the range of 150 million euros a day, and voices in the industry were starting to denounce the mess that we, Europe—Europe, always Europe—had made by being overcautious. Was it reasonable to reopen the airways as of tomorrow morning? Manfred Hübner said he had no idea, and that in any case it wasn't up to us, but rather to the civil aviation authorities of the various countries. To each his burning issue, to each his volcanic ash. Our role was to continue gathering reliable information from all of the concerned sectors, the makers of reactors (Rolls-Royce, General Electric, Pratt & Whitney), the airplane manufacturers, the airlines, and of course the Volcanic Ash Advisory Centre (VAAC), the meteorological observatory in charge of collecting such information. At last report, three-quarters of Europe was still in the cloud zone, and there was nothing to suggest that the eruption of Eyjafjöll was going to subside in the coming days. For the moment, it was impossible to predict how long it would last, several days or a year. The floor then went to the director of air transports, Miguel Cordoba. He spoke firmly, in English that bore a slight trace of a Castilian accent. The fact is, we in Europe are utterly helpless when faced with such a situation, he said. But there are certain countries, such as Indonesia, that are confronted frequently with this type of volcanic activity and have long had specific protocols in place to deal with them. We might learn from their experience. Those countries have set up a surveillance system to manage risk and have established certain standards. As for us, we are currently incapable of answering the two basic questions that would determine whether air traffic can resume: How much volcanic ash can a reactor withstand? And what concentration of particles per cubic meter can a plane fly through safely? That said, we do know that no tolerance threshold can be established in the absolute. I'll give you an example. Let's say we've established that an aircraft can fly safely for *two minutes* in a cloud of volcanic ash: that doesn't mean that those two minutes are an absolute norm, for it depends on the concentration of ash the plane is flying through. If the concentration is high, even two minutes might pose a real threat. We therefore need not only precise information on the reactors' tolerance threshold, but also accurate charts showing the concentration levels for every relevant geographic area. On this last point, we should turn to Eurocontrol, the only agency that has access to all the available information and can act as intermediary between the political sphere and experts on the ground, he concluded, taking a slug of coffee from his plastic cup. It was a shrewd move on his part: without seeming to, he had put the burden on Eurocontrol. Relations between the Commission and Eurocontrol had always been difficult. The Commission felt it had sole power to shape policy and that Eurocontrol was simply there to execute, while Eurocontrol jealously guarded its autonomy. In reality the Commission was caught between two untenable positions: We could either stand firm against pressure from the airlines and keep the airways closed until we had sufficient safety guarantees, or we could reopen the airways as early as the following morning, at considerable risk of exposing ourselves to an incident. If we reopened the airways and a single airplane had a serious accident or had to make an emergency landing due to volcanic ash, the Commission would be held responsible, especially if people were injured. The optics would have been disastrous. And if there was even one casualty, we'd never recover. In the blink of an eye, the same people who had been yowling for the skies to reopen would be calling us irresponsible and blaming us for playing with public safety, and once again it would be the Commission's fault, Brussels's fault, Europe's fault. On the other hand, the economic influence of the airlines, and the mammoth support they gave the member states, dictated that we couldn't keep the skies closed indefinitely. For the Commission, these were the stakes at issue today. We were touching on the very essence of political decision-making, having to choose between two impossible positions.

After the meeting, I barely had time to stop in my office before five of us left for the Berlaymont, where we had an appointment with Commissioner Kallas. For the past three days, we had gone from one emergency session to the next, in a bustle of activity and the headiness of being at the center of events. We hastened up Rue Breydel, surrounding our director, our arms laden with folders. At the Berlaymont, we rushed through security and took the elevators. Commissioner Kallas had a spacious office on the eleventh floor, with a large bay window that filtered the light through shaded glass blinds. When we entered, he was sitting at the back of the room, at his work table, in a video conference with the president of the European Parliament's Committee on Transport and Tourism. Without getting up or breaking stride (he continued listening to his interlocutor onscreen), he made a sweeping gesture with his arm for us to come in and make ourselves comfortable. We took seats on the black sofa and the three or four armchairs placed around a coffee table. In the adjoining office, through an open door, we could see his chief of staff on the phone. When Siim Kallas finished his conversation, he stood up, put his suit jacket back on, and came to join us. He explained that pressure on the Commission to reopen the airways was becoming untenable. The airlines were growing more insistent, and the International Air Transport Association had just issued a press release demanding an immediate reevaluation of the flight restrictions so that at least several airways could reopen. Even the press was getting into the act, starting to criticize us for excessive caution. Pensively leafing through a file that our director had handed him, he added that there was a golden rule he had often observed, which was that public opinion tended not to accept safety measures for events that were unlikely to occur. That's how it is, he said, knowing at the same time how easily public opinion could turn against us. He laid the file on the table, stood up, and left us alone for a moment. He had gone into the neighboring office, where we saw him exchange a few words with his chief of staff regarding his departure for Eurocontrol.

We were due at Eurocontrol at two p.m. The meeting at the Berlaymont came to an end. I was putting my coat back on, and I had moved toward the bay window. I looked outside, past the glass strips of the blinds. Down below was Rue de la Loi, where very few cars were visible on a Sunday morning. Across the way rose the outline of the Justus Lipsius, with its glass and pink granite façade. I was on the eleventh floor of the Berlaymont, in the office of the Commission vice president, and I was thinking about my father, who would never know the joy of having an office in the renovated building. My father was in the hospital that day. He had had a lung operation a week and a half earlier. Shortly before that, during a routine checkup, he had learned that his tests results were bad and that he'd need surgery. I hadn't gone to see him these past days, had barely had time to call, but he was recovering well, having always had a strong constitution. A mere three days after the surgery, when Pierre and I had gone to visit him in the hospital, he proved to us that he'd lost none of his combativeness. The name of the hospital was Erasme (my father must have appreciated being under the protection of his dear Erasmus—he couldn't be in better hands). It was the previous Sunday afternoon, exactly one week before. When we'd entered his room, we had found him sitting up in his pajamas, motionless, pale, with an IV in his wrist, and staring silently at the ceiling. We stayed with him for nearly an hour. Pierre sat on a chair at the foot of the bed, and I stood by the window, staring out at the hospital's gray parking structure. Pierre was just back from China, where he'd gone on business (he had been lucky enough to sneak through Eyjafjöll), and he was telling my father how impressed he'd been by the dynamism of Chinese architecture, and more generally by the dynamism of Chinese society, its youth and the opportunities for women, citing the example of a female construction foreperson barely forty years old, who was in charge of more than two thousand workers on the site of the new museum in Shanghai. I had heartily agreed, and Pierre had lauded the richness of China's thousand-year-old civilization. At that point, his patience at an end, my father had abruptly interrupted our panegyric by paraphrasing de Gaulle: "Yes, of course, you can jump up in your chair like a goat crying 'China! China! China!' but it will lead nowhere and means nothing!" We had been surprised by the vehemence of his reaction. Sitting on his bed, face pale, irritated by the enthusiasm we were showing for China, he had reminded us, his eyes somber, with visible emotion, short of breath and in an altered voice, about the thousands of dead in Tiananmen Square, the arbitrary arrests, the violations of human rights that continued to be commonplace. Neither my brother nor I could be accused of complacency toward attacks on democracy (our father was, after all, our father), but, once you got past those reservations—which we admitted were considerable—we looked enthusiastically upon the formidable creative energy of China in the early 2010s, the dynamism of its society, and even the breath of freedom that seemed to be blowing through the spheres of arts and technological innovation. But my father saw only the political side, the repression of lawyers, the lack of journalistic freedom. And for me, that's redhibitory, he said with a closed expression, both weakened by illness and furious at the turn the conversation had taken. Sitting up in his bed, aghast, he couldn't get over the fact that his two grown sons should defy him on a matter that touched on the defense of human rights. Even if, in theory, he could admit that our opinions might differ from his—intellectually, he could even accept such a thing—in reality, he couldn't tolerate it.

We left the Berlaymont to go to the headquarters of Eurocontrol in Diegem. There was almost no traffic in the streets, and we drove in a convoy up Boulevard Léopold III. I had never yet set foot in Eurocontrol, but the way was familiar, it was the same as to get to Zaventem Airport. I didn't say a word in the car but peered through the window at the sky over Brussels, a vast, empty sky, almost cloudless. It didn't matter which way we went, as far as the eye could see there was not a single airplane, from the Atlantic coast to the Urals, the Mediterranean to Scandinavia. The sky had suddenly become deserted and silent. It had been forty-eight hours since a flight had taken off in Northern Europe, and I thought about the hundreds of planes stalled on the tarmac of the empty airports. I thought about the perishable foodstuffs piled up in refrigerated warehouses in the freight zones, the wilting flowers, the crates of rotting fruit, the tons of fresh fish that had to be destroyed in the Zaventem hangars. I thought about the organs intended for human transplants whose deliveries were on hold, delayed, or blocked; I thought about the sporting and cultural events that had to be canceled, about the hundreds of thousands of passengers suffering all over the world. I thought about all this, and it came home to me that working for Europe had a concrete meaning, a palpable significance. What I was doing, what my colleagues and I were doing at the Commission, suddenly had a material and tangible impact on citizens' lives. I thought about the responsibility we had, today, at our level, to represent Europe, to be one of the cogs, and how necessary it was to prove ourselves worthy, to be up to the task, to banish the erroneous perceptions of Europe as hobbled, rigid, technocratic, abstract. Hadn't we, in less than two days, and *pace* the populists, restored the sky to the birds?

Sitting in the back of the car, I opened the Flightradar24 app on my phone, which followed the progress of commercial flights in real time. I had chosen Zaventem Airport on the map and, seeing no flights leaving or approaching it, I had widened my search to show all of Belgium, the Netherlands, and the southern part of Great Britain, the strategic crossroads of Northern Europe, where normally speaking you would see hundreds of tiny yellow icons of stylized airplanes swarming around the map like insects, teeming in tangled concentrations about Heathrow or Schiphol. At present, there wasn't a single aircraft in the area, not one yellow icon on my screen. Amazed, I had shown the image to Miguel Cordoba sitting next to me; impressed in turn, he had leaned toward my phone and zoomed out with two fingers to widen the search area, looking for a plane. Not finding any, somewhat concerned, he had further widened the search, until he finally came across the first icons of planes in flight in the far south of Europe.

Our convoy had exited the highway, and we were driving by the secured entrances to NATO headquarters. The car passed through a barrier, slowed down, and entered a narrow path before coming out onto a large court, its central esplanade bristling with flags. Several official vehicles were already parked in front of the glass entrance of Eurocontrol headquarters. We were greeted by the organization's head of Communications, who escorted us down the glassed-in hallways and into the control room, where dozens of air traffic controllers leaning over their screens verified flight paths from the plans they'd received. Because so many airways had been closed, there were intense areas of congestion on the borders of the no-fly zone, and the controllers had to help airlines confronting this novel situation to find alternate routes, given the restrictions. Every workstation in the vast control room was occupied. Lined up in dozens of rows, the controllers were wearing headphones with mics, which allowed them to engage in hundreds of conversations simultaneously while not interfering with others in the room. The Communications director led us to a huge wall screen, divided into various quadrants and windows, with air traffic maps that were updating in real time. It immediately showed the seriousness of the crisis and the extent of flight cancellations, as not a single dot symbolized the presence of an aircraft over the entire territory of the United Kingdom.

There was confusion, bustle, and even some jostling to get to the conference room where the emergency meeting with the Spanish minister of transportation was being held. (At the time, it was Spain's turn to preside over the European Union.) After a few words of welcome, the CEO of Eurocontrol got down to business. He explained that, for the past two days, at the Commission's request, he and his teams had been discussing possible solutions to the crisis, and that today he was able to offer three options. The first was to maintain the status quo: the Northern European skies would remain closed, no risk of accidents because no flights. That was the safest. The second was the Ameri can approach, a rather liberal procedure that consisted in leaving the decision of whether or not to fly to the airlines themselves, with no government intervention. I understood that this was clearly not the option preferred by Eurocontrol, as you can hardly call an option the "American approach" if you want to sell it to politicians charged with defining a European position. In any case, it was untenable for Europe, which would have looked like it was washing its hands of the problem. The third option was an intermediary approach, in which Eurocontrol made recommendations but left the final decision to the state governments. It was this latter option that was adopted, with little debate or disagreement, though everyone chimed in nonetheless with a word or analysis to explain why this seemed the most apt. The matter having been settled, the floor went to Ian Maloney, the man in charge of forecasting for Eurocontrol, who was to detail the way that recommendations would actually be carried out. He went to the magnetic whiteboard, picked up a red marker, and told us that Eurocontrol had divided European airspace into three distinct zones, depending on the concentration of ash from Eyjafjöll, and he wrote the names of the three zones on the board as he said them. Zone A: forbidden zone, risk high enough that we recommend maintaining flight restrictions. Zone B: precaution zone, with lower particle density, in which planes can be authorized or banned, at the discretion of the member states. Zone C: open zone, in which the risk is considered negligible.

After the meeting broke up, there was a moment of hesitation, a pause in the afternoon; we left the room as if the meeting was going to resume after a break, and the delegations didn't immediately disperse. Throughout the hallway, small groups of people were huddled together, while others were sitting on the floor with computers on their laps. Some had gone outside to smoke, and through the window I saw the Spanish minister and his bodyguard in conversation in an inner courtyard. Some officials were giving interviews: you could see them standing, answering reporters' questions for the TV cameras. Sometimes the name Eyjafjöll cropped up, and even Eyjafjallajökull, for those who were more knowledgeable or more pedantic. For it was important not to confuse Eyjafjöll and Eyjafjallajökull. I remembered a discussion about the name of the volcano on the first day of the crisis between Manfred Hübner and an expert who had paid an urgent visit to our offices. Eyjafjallajökull is the name of the glacier, the expert had explained, a vast ice cap in the south of Iceland. The volcano itself was called Eyjafjöll. Or more precisely, the Eyjafjölls, he had continued, since it was a massif with several volcanoes. Let's not complicate matters, our CEO had said, knitting his brow. For convenience's sake, I suggest that, from now on, whenever we mention the volcano in an official document, we use Eyjafjöll. Let's keep it simple.

I looked for a place to sit and revise the GRI report, based on what had just been said in the meeting. There were no free places, so I went back into the control room. I walked between the tables, laptop in hand, looking for an unoccupied seat. I ended up spotting a chair, which I dragged behind me, and set up shop at the end of a table. I asked a controller with my eyes if it was all right to sit there, and without a word he opened his hand to invite me to take a seat. I put my laptop on the table, entered my password in the login screen to get a secure internet connection. I picked up my email, of which I'd received about a dozen since that morning. One was from Elisabetta, which I opened immediately. She had just woken up in Los Angeles, where she and Alessandro had been stuck for two days. The

Air France flight they were scheduled to take had again been canceled, and for the moment they were staying in the airport hotel. Elisabetta was thrilled, delighted to be able to prolong her stay, and Alessandro was being lovely. She had even taken advantage of the hotel swimming pool, and was, in a word, swimming in delight. Her email ended: "I'm so happy!" (She was the first person I'd met since the beginning of the crisis who was enthusiastic about the eruption of Eyjafjöll.)

Sitting at my corner of the table in the control room, I had typed two phrases into my computer, "Third option, intermediate approach based on guidance from Eurocontrol" and "Maintenance of final decision to member states," and I pondered how to synthesize these two pieces of news into a single intelligible sentence. I was turning the wording over in my head when a young woman I hadn't noticed came up behind me and asked if I knew the Eurocontrol Wi-Fi password. She must have guessed, seeing me perched at my corner of the table, that I wasn't part of the crew, and she had asked me so as not to disturb the controllers who were hard at work. The Eurocontrol Wi-Fi password was a basic code, which hadn't been changed. Miguel Cordoba had given it to me, and I saw no reason to keep it secret. It's a bit complicated, I said. I had jotted down the code on a piece of paper, which I now took from my pocket and started to read to her, giving her time to enter, one by one, the long string of uppercase letters, lowercase letters, numbers, punctuation marks, and mathematical signs. I saw her standing behind me, concentrating, pressing with one finger on her phone's keypad: g<d/Zq4B>&YwF/2Ui2N. Having successfully entered the code, she thanked me, and we chatted some more about the Eyjafjöll crisis. I pointed out that she had a slight accent when she said "Eyjafjöll." She smiled. That's true, I'm not Icelandic, you're very observant. But even in English, I said (for that's what we were speaking), you have a slight accent. Don't tell me, let me guess. You wouldn't be Spanish, by any chance? She overplayed her astonishment (Incredible! How did you guess!) and gave me one last smile before walking away. She walked while looking at her phone, already connected to the internet, and I saw her go into the hall toward the conference room. I finished my sentence for the GRI report, which I typed into my laptop: "While leaving the member states the ultimate decision as to whether to reopen their airspace, it was decided, based on existing technical studies and constantly updated data from Eurocontrol, to split European airspace into three separate zones, depending on the concentration of ash emitted by Eyjafjöll." I inserted the sentence into the third section of the GRI report (proposed course of action), and I sent it in a group email to my contacts in the various commissioners' offices. All this was fairly routine; I didn't expect anyone to raise any objections, but I preferred to get everyone's consent as of that evening to avoid any setbacks the next morning, when the chiefs of staff were scheduled to validate the GRI report.

I was heading back toward the conference room when I ran into Miguel Cordoba in the hall. He was a true regular of the place and knew everyone here. He was with Ian Maloney, the forecasting head who had spoken at the meeting, and with a flight captain from KLM who had been brought into the crisis management team because of his practical experience with flying in volcanic zones. Ian Maloney was about to show them the offices and invited me to join. He slid a magnetic card in an electronic lock to open a double glass door, and we entered the restricted zone, where the staff offices were located. I realized, seeing all the hectic activity on this Sunday afternoon, that if we, in DG MOVE, had been on deck since midweek, it was nothing compared to Eurocontrol, which had been placed on maximum alert. Ian Maloney hadn't left his office in three days; he slept on-site and had only been back home for an hour the day before to shower. The heads of Eurocontrol had assigned him to make detailed charts of particle concentration, which were posted every six hours on the organization's web portal. He ushered us into his office, where three people were busy at their computers. On the tables, some fifty retouched and corrected charts were stacked up next to a jumble of colored markers and ballpoints. There was a folding cot against the wall, a coffee maker, a few dirty dishes abandoned on a cabinet. Ian Maloney picked up a chart and, standing in the middle of the room, he commented on it, detailing how he had drawn them up. For the initial charts, had had added safety zones of sixty nautical miles, marked in red, so as to take no risks. Leaning over the chart, the KLM pilot nodded in approval. As he saw it, the extreme danger posed by the ash was still being underestimated. You have to understand that volcanic ash is not like regular dust, he said. It's very abrasive, hard and sharp like glass shards. If an airplane takes in sand, it's not really a problem, it will simply be ejected by the reactor, but volcanic ash is liable to fuse in the reactor and form concretions that can obstruct the engines. It's what happened with the British Airways Boeing 747 in the famous Jakarta incident, the four engines failed simultaneously. The aircraft was able to glide for another fifteen minutes but, at 13,500 feet, the engines still weren't working, and the crew prepared to set down on the Indian Ocean—you can imagine what it's like to land on water with a 747, it had never been attempted before and never has been since. Finally, some of the engines restarted and the Boeing was able to make an emergency landing in Jakarta. But the plane had been so badly damaged that it had to be towed to the terminal—its windscreen was blackened and streaked with ash.

Soon we gathered for our return to the Berlaymont. A press conference had been set for six o'clock to report on the Eurocontrol meeting. In the car, I thought about the pilot's alarmist comments: for the moment, given the lack of a precise definition of safe concentration of ash for the various types of engines, he didn't see who could give a reliable authorization for takeoff, nor what the criteria would be. He told us that, the day before, Lufthansa had flown an empty plane with sensors into the cloud, and that two other test flights were scheduled for today, a KLM from Amsterdam to Dusseldorf, and an Air France from Paris to Toulouse. Test flights are fine, he said, but we shouldn't risk letting passengers fly. I thought about those words and felt a diffuse anxiety spread through me. I had a bad premonition.

Arriving at the Berlaymont, I immediately went to the press room. Instead of sitting toward the front, I took a seat in back, away from the others, so that I could quietly slip out if need be. More than a hundred reporters were in the room, walking down the aisles and calling out to each other in the rows of seats, exchanging signs of greeting in the commotion. At the foot of the podium, several TV crews had already set up their tripods. At exactly six p.m., Commission Vice President Kallas and the Spanish transportation minister came onstage through a hidden door in the back. Each went to stand behind a podium, while the photographers at the foot of the stage aimed their telephotos at the scene. Vice President Kallas greeted the audience and began reading his notes in a hoarse voice. We are faced with an unprecedented shutdown of Europe's airspace, he said. Never before has such a large area of the skyway been closed, and closed for some time to come, according to the weather forecasts. The situation is not sustainable. It is now clear that we cannot just wait until the ash cloud dissipates. Over the last two days, the European Commission, with the assistance of Eurocontrol, has held a series of intensive meetings. There are three key principles we are basing our work on: First, there can be no compromise on safety; safety is our top priority. We're working to find solutions so that we can maximize available airspace without compromising safety. Second, the economic consequences. In the coming days, I shall be leading a group of experts to find solutions and analyze the economic consequences of the crisis, for the air travel industry and Europe in general. Third, passengers. This was the departure point of our thinking, how to deal with the losses suffered by hundreds of thousands of passengers whose flights have been canceled. I was listening only distractedly to Vice President Kallas, as I knew all of this by heart, when suddenly something he said snapped me back to attention. He said: "These are very difficult decisions to make, as passengers' lives are at stake." On the surface, it was a neutral, innocuous sentence, but it suddenly brought home to me what all of this meant, that the lives of passengers were hanging in the balance. Again I was filled with that sense of anxiety that I had felt in the car. I've always had that worry dormant in me, general and widespread, ready to reactivate at the slightest alert. What until then had been only a vague, unexpressed impression suddenly crystallized in my mind and became an obsessive dread. I again began to fear, however irrationally, that if air traffic resumed today, we could be facing an aviation disaster.

I left the press room. I needed some air, and a shot of coffee. I had my phone with me and was checking the latest news, when suddenly I stopped dead in the hall. I had just read exactly what I'd hoped not to read, that restrictions had been relaxed and that airports in the South of France had reopened. Flights were being scheduled for that same evening from Nice and Marseilles. I hadn't felt afraid of flying for some time, but suddenly that terror came rushing back, though in a peculiar way. I wasn't afraid for myself, or even for my loved ones, but in absolute terms, abstractly: I was terrified that tonight there would be an air disaster in Europe. I had just come in sight of the cafeteria. The place was quiet, almost empty, with some potted plants and two or three people sitting at tables in a tranquil décor. I remembered the state the place had been in when I'd visited it ten years earlier with my brother, the infernal noise, the darkness and dust, the chthonian shadows haunting the unlit space of the cafeteria under construction. I poured myself a coffee from the machine and put it on a tray, but I couldn't banish from my mind the images of destruction and devastation that pursued me as I envisioned the rubble of a plane crash. I imagined the atmosphere here, in the Berlaymont, if tonight or tomorrow, after the airways reopened, we learned that a plane had gone down—a plane that had at first lost contact, and then, after unbearable suspended hours of waiting in which the most insane rumors and suppositions flew, the worst was finally announced, and we had confirmation that the plane that had gone silent had indeed crashed, and that the most likely cause was volcanic ash in the engines.

I was walking into the cafeteria, holding my tray, lost in thought, when I noticed, sitting alone at a table, the young woman to whom I'd given the Eurocontrol Wi-Fi code earlier that afternoon. She recognized me and waved. I headed toward her, and she invited me to sit at her table. I sat down and we started speaking in French (she had switched to French once she realized that it was my native tongue). Her French was as fluent as her English, and she wasn't sorry to leave behind the language that she used all day long for her work and that was now associated in her mind with the Eyjafjöll crisis. She told me she'd just come from the press room, that she needed to take a break, to stop for a moment, that her life had been put on hold these past five days because of the Icelandic volcano. She couldn't get any sleep, she didn't even know how she found the time to eat, and she showed me the nearly empty plate of salad on her tray. She kept going on coffee, which she drank all day long, and she stood up to go get another. She asked if I'd like one as well. I hadn't yet touched my coffee, which she must have noticed, and yet she offered me one. I didn't answer immediately. I looked her in the eye, and I thought that if I said yes, that "yes" could have repercussions much more unexpected than I could have imagined. She waited, holding my gaze, with an imperceptible smile playing about her lips. So is that a yes? Yes, I said. I watched her head off toward the counter. I don't know at what moment I told myself that she was very attractive, and I'm not even sure I ever did, or in any case not in those terms. Her name was Pilar Alcantara. She'd lived in Brussels for eight years, worked at the Permanent Representation of Spain to the European Union. For the past two days, she had been following the delegation of the Spanish transportation minister. I watched her from a distance as she paid at the register. She came back holding a tray on which twin coffees were posed side by side. She sat down and set my second coffee next to the first, with a slight smile and a challenging expression. We each took a sip of coffee, not two, just a single sip, and then there was a look, a new exchange of glances, nothing more, simple, straightforward, intent, obvious, and without a word, without our knowing how, we found ourselves holding hands. While there had been so many women in my life who had filled my thoughts for weeks or months before I dared tell them how I felt, with Pilar Alcantara I had simply exchanged a calm, assured glance and found myself holding hands with her, when I didn't even know who she was, had never given her a thought before today, had never imagined anything between us, any conversation, any caress. Our hands remained joined for a moment, and then, as naturally as they had found each other, they regained their freedom and their autonomy. This unexpected circumstance, of taking one another's hands, hampered the rest of our conversation, complicated it, hindered it; we could sense a kind of latent awkwardness lurking beneath the generalities that we continued to bat back and forth about the eruption of Eyjafjöll. We were talking just to fill the silence; it was now our eyes, and them alone, that, picking up where our hands had left off, pursued the true dialogue between us, the exchange of tenderness that we felt burgeoning. I looked at her and I could feel something happening, something happening to me. It's a singular virtue of love to make us feel that what's happening is happening to us and no one else—that the glance addressed, the gesture half made, is for us and us alone; and the feeling of election that this truth procures brings with it an intense sense of well-being that instantly makes everything else disappear, tiredness and professional cares, evil premonitions and dread. We finished our coffees and stood up to return our trays. After sliding them into the superimposed racks, our hands, free again, drawn to each other, waiting for each other, seeking each other, united once more, and, in the same movement, the same impulse, irrepressibly, our bodies joined, and we embraced there, next to the stainless steel rails of the cafeteria's self-service counter.

It was a flicker. In that instant, that second, in the joining of our bodies, the contact of the other's body against one's own, we slipped out of our lives. Forgotten were our daily round, our habits, our routines; forgotten our fatigue, proprieties and obligations, flight restrictions, Eyjafjöll, the

GRI report. We had only one thought in our heads, to get out of there, leave that place, flee the poisonous atmosphere and the thoughts we'd been mulling for the past five days, abandon the Berlaymont, the press conference, Vice President Kallas, the Spanish transport minister, deliver us from the anxieties that had built up since the beginning of the crisis, leave all of that behind and run away hand in hand through the streets of Brussels. We left the cafeteria and crossed the foyer of the Berlaymont toward the exit. But we stopped short, our momentum halted. Through the windows of the main entrance, we saw several official vehicles parked on the courtyard, their drivers waiting, and security personnel who seemed to be blocking our path. We turned back, hoping to exit the building more discreetly, by a less frequented route. I knew the place well, and I pulled Pilar Alcantara behind me toward the VIP entrance in the north wing; as it was no doubt deserted on a Sunday evening, we could slip out quietly to Rue Stevin. I used my badge to pass through the security doors, having access to all the restricted areas of the building. We had taken a new hallway, and we rushed through an empty waiting room reserved for visiting personalities. But after we passed through other security doors, I got a bit lost and wasn't sure where I was. We climbed a short flight of stairs and followed a corridor, at the end of which was a door. I swung it open, expecting to come out into the atrium leading to the VIP entrance, and we suddenly found ourselves onstage, in the middle of the press conference. The door I had just opened was a mere several feet behind the speakers' podiums. I could feel in front of me the almost palpable physical presence of the Spanish minister of transportation, who was delivering his talk. Pilar Alcantara, who was following close behind, bumped into me when I stopped short; she put her hand on my shoulder, but I was already closing the door, having opened and shut it again practically in the same motion, the instant I'd realized my mistake. I had taken only one step onto the stage, not even a full step, but in that brief second I had seen everyone's eyes converge on me. Vice President Kallas had jerked his head around, startled that someone should suddenly appear at his back. He knew me, knew who I was, and I had read the puzzlement in his eyes, the stupefaction. In the split second that the stage door was open, I had also made eye contact with the Spanish transport minister, who had interrupted himself, dumbfounded, then tried to pick up where he left off, his sentence hanging in the void, struggling to regain the thread of what he'd been saying. In the instant that I'd remained in the open doorway, I had seen a wave of agitation shudder throughout the front rows of the audience. I don't know if they were reporters or security staff, but I saw people stand, leave their seats and rush toward the stage or the wings. For not only had the entire press corps seen that door open, but so had the security team, which was always on the lookout for unexpected occurrences, ready to react to the slightest anomaly, to leap from their seats to intervene: it's their job to predict the impossible, anticipate the unlikely, even if that backstage door was the last place they expected to see danger, that ultra-secure door used by officials when taking the podium, a door accessible to duly authorized personnel only. I knew we were being chased and, turning back with Pilar Alcantara, picking up our pace in the hallways, almost running, we again landed in the main atrium of the

Berlaymont, where it was impossible to hide or find the slightest recess. We turned desperately around the atrium, and it felt as though we were being observed from the high walkways above: two tiny, panic-stricken silhouettes in that imposing glass architecture, desperate to escape the trap that was closing around them but constantly running up against sealed panes of glass, not knowing where to turn, which door to open, what hallway to run down. It was as if we were surrounded by a raging fire, danger on all sides—and it was then that I suddenly remembered the underground passageway Pierre had shown me during that visit ten years earlier. I didn't know if it still existed, whether it was still open or had been blocked off, if it was surveilled, or even if we could get through it, but I immediately began searching for it. I pulled Pilar after me in the service stairs and we headed for the underground parking levels, third level down, then the fourth. We descended ever more deeply into the bowels of the Berlaymont, down to Level -5. I recognized the way, I knew where I was. We passed through a door and ran through the parking garage, sticking close to the concrete pillars. Skirting around a guard booth, I opened a heavy fire door, and we entered the secret passage.

The tunnel was in even greater disrepair than I remembered it, with puddles of water dotting the tiny walkway and uneven walls sweating dampness, lead pipes and conduits running along the ceiling. Pilar Alcantara walked beside me in the underground passage. I could make out her anxious face in the semidarkness. Most of the pilot lights had burned out. We saw a yellowish glow at the other end of the tunnel, like a semaphore, trembling, vacillating, short of breath, and suddenly that signal went out and we were plunged into darkness. We inched our way forward, slowly, down the unlit corridor. Pilar Alcantara took my hand out of fear, but the moment our hands came in contact, the moment our skin touched, our bodies came together and joined once again. We stopped in the dark, interlaced, to catch our breath; then, huddled together, saying nothing, we listened to the sounds in the distance, straining to hear any possible pursuers. The press conference must have resumed upstairs. Anyway, it had never really stopped, there had been no break in the session, only a pause, a splinter in the immutable and imperturbable course of events. Perhaps a member of the security team had climbed onstage to make sure no one was lurking behind the door, or perhaps they had verified from the other side so that the reporters wouldn't see. No doubt they had rushed to the control room to check the images from the surveillance cameras, perhaps had frozen the image at the moment of the incident, my halted body and petrified expression forever captured onscreen. We had resumed moving forward, continued to follow the narrow walkway in the dark without hearing any noises other than the faraway echoes of a highway tunnel in which cars and trucks rumbled underground. When I opened the fire door at the other end, we were dazzled by the daylight. We climbed a narrow staircase and came out the other side, in the entrance foyer of the Justus Lipsius building. We were immediately surrounded by security personnel. I thought it was the Berlaymont security agents who had crossed the street to meet us when we emerged from the tunnel, but they were Justus Lipsius security. They weren't aware of anything, simply wanted to know what we were doing there. I showed them my badge. They examined it, asked a few questions. My answers seemed to satisfy them. They kept us there for another few moments, just to run a routine check, then let us leave. We caught a cab on Rue de la Loi.

I wasn't sure where we were going—we'd decide where to get out when we got there. The taxi drove along the Brussels streets. I was out of breath, could feel my heart pounding in my chest, and I felt intensely alive in that cab next to Pilar Alcantara, who was pressed against me on the back seat. She was squeezed against my shoulder, and I sensed the ardor of her presence beside me. She leaned over to my ear and whispered, "You want me." It wasn't really a question, she hadn't asked if I wanted her—as if she could have doubted it for a minute—but neither was it, or not exactly, the equivalent of "I want you." She had said, "You want me," and it could have been read as at once a question and an admission, her "You want me" containing both "Do you want me?" and "I want you," but she had said neither, and there remained a share of irreducible mystery in her formulation. It was the first time she had explicitly brought up the matter of sexual attraction. You want me, she repeated, as if the danger from which we'd just escaped had keened her desire, and in a flash I understood what she meant by "You want me." It wasn't a question, it was a reply. What she meant was, "Yes, you want me, I know it, I know you want me." It was an observation, a burning, pressing, imperious observation: that I wanted her, that she could see it, and that it thrilled her. I placed my hand on her thigh, and immediately, in the first contact of my fingers on the fabric of her translucent black tights, I had to face the obvious: yes, I wanted her, there was no question that I wanted her.

But I also knew, or I knew later, with certainty, that my desire to touch her and be touched by her, the irrepressible need we had to unite our bodies as soon as possible, had an explanation that went beyond us; that what we were experiencing, beyond the attraction we felt for one another, was the result of all the tensions we had built up in the past five days. It was anxiety and dread that had thrown us into each other's arms. After the September 11 attacks, studies had shown that New Yorkers, in reaction to the extreme violence of the stress they'd experienced, had felt an exacerbated need to couple. My encounter with Pilar Alcantara was the fruit of exceptional circumstances, which probably wouldn't have happened otherwise, and I realized that the intense hours we were living through were but a consequence, perhaps the sweetest consequence, not to say the most unexpected, of the eruption of Eyjafjöll thousands of miles away.

We had reached the center of town, and I asked the taxi driver to drop us at the entrance to the Royal Galleries. We got out of the car and went in search of a hotel, going into the first one we saw, an impersonal hotel, part of an international chain. We went to the reception desk and asked for a room, everything went smoothly, before we knew it we were in the elevator, and soon she was naked in my arms, and we were embracing passionately on the hotel bed. We had hardly pulled down the covers, our clothes lay in a jumble around us. With my eyes closed, I ran my hands over her body, felt her hands on my skin. I discovered her hips, the heaviness of her breasts. She stopped and looked at me. Lying next to me on the bed, bringing her face close to mine, her hand on my cheek, she kissed me, and, feeling her tongue in my mouth for the first time, I understood that this was the first time we had kissed. Since our first meeting, constantly buffeted by circumstances, we hadn't had the opportunity. It felt as if we'd been waiting for this kiss for an eternity, since the moment we'd sensed it approaching, the moment we'd known for a certainty that its time would come, as if we'd been awaiting it for centuries. We kissed in a frenzy, and I couldn't believe the unforeseen turn the day had taken. From the moment I'd met her, in a single movement, a single breath, inhaled continuously in a whirlwind of vertigo and emotions, I had simultaneously known attraction and apprehension, desire and fear, love and dread.